To Lauren

Sweet Girl

Jack Whitney

For my main bitch, Kay

Because this short literally would not have been possible without you.
Thank you for bringing these two into my life, and for always pushing me out of my comfort zone and into terrifying places.

Sweet Girl's content warning is short and sweet.

This novella is not intended for anyone under the age of eighteen.

This novella features graphic sexual activities between two consenting adults. No acts in this novella are in any way meant as a guide to exploring sexual fantasies or to give suggestions.

Sweet Girl contains the following subjects in addition to the graphic sexual activity:
Explicit language and brief mentions of loss/grief and implied self-harm

This is a work of fiction.

Enjoy.

"Hey, Gav." One of the decorators chucked a small package towards him "This was left at the office."

Gavin caught it just as the bartender slid him a sample of one of the signature drinks for the singles event that night—a pomegranate martini. Gavin took a sip as he read the note on the box.

Try to behave tonight.

He recognized the handwriting—had stared at it on packages for more than a millennia, most of the time only on Valentine's Day, though. This one was no different. It was gift from his mother, probably something boring with instructions to keep his usual mischievous pranks to a minimum.

Gavin tossed the box over his shoulder and into the trash.

"What do you think?" the bartender asked him about the drink.

"Keep these coming to me later," he told her.

Valentine's Day was Gavin's favorite day of the year. He loved it. *Reveled* in it. He'd grown away from striking strangers with arrows to toy with their emotions in his godly form long ago. Now, he used his skills to lure strangers together using something much more potent than any arrow he'd ever let fly: a dating app he'd created called Cupid's Arrow.

His phone buzzed. Another RSVP claimed.

He chuckled under his breath at the triumph and pushed his phone back in his pocket, looking up in time to see the banner being strung across the ceiling.

As if everyone attending the party wasn't fully aware of the dating app sponsoring it.

"Hey, Av," he called to the coordinator.

Avril, the event coordinator, was standing across the bar room, instructing the two on the bartop whether to go up or down with the banner. She was fantastic at her job and one of his favorite people at the company; a middle-aged woman who he adored teasing with since she was always game for whatever he had ideas for.

"Yes, Cupid?" Avril called back. "You know, you don't have to be here," she added.

Every time someone used the name, it amused him, unbeknownst to them that he was actually Cupid. *Eros*. The god himself. They all thought they were clever, giving him the nickname when he'd come up with the elaborate dating app years back.

It was fucking adorable.

Hands in his pockets, Gavin made his way through the sea of tables and chairs to stand by her side. He reached for a dish of naughty candy hearts that they'd had made for the event, and he popped one that read '*DTF*' into his mouth.

"A little up on the left—Sarah, was that a little, really?" Avril was saying.

"Do you think anyone will guess who's sponsoring the party?" he said to her in a low tone.

Avril glared sideways, her neck craning to look up at him from her short stature. "You hate it."

He popped another heart back. "A little ostentatious," he said, the corner of his lip lifting just so.

Avril was still staring at him as though she was ready to

punch his face in, and he couldn't help giving her a crooked smirk, a dimple beneath his short ginger scruff shining. Her lips twisted at the sight of his mockery, and Avril huffed.

"It's a good thing you're cute," she muttered. "Take it down!" Avril announced, and the entire room stood still. But Avril was already gathering up some of the more obnoxious decorations. "Scale it back by half," she added, her brow raising at Gavin as she snatched up things left and right into a rolling trash bin.

She grabbed one of the bowls of candy hearts, and Gavin grabbed her wrist.

"Those stay," he told her.

The frustration slipped from her expression, and a smile lifted in her eyes instead. "Oh, he likes the naughty hearts," she teased.

"Could be fun," he mused before picking up another.

GOOD GIRL, it read.

Avril chuckled softly as she crumbled up one of the heart papers. "The god has spoken," she said loudly to the decorating crew. "Leave the candies, the roses, and the confetti on the tables. Toss the rest of it."

Gavin held Avril's—only slightly annoyed—gaze a moment, and then he slid the candy heart in her direction. She read it with knitted brows, nearly rolling her eyes, but unable to stifle her widening grin. Gavin gave her a wink and turned on his heel.

"See you in an hour, Av," he called back. He circled, walking backward, saying, "You should wear something more fitting on those curves. Show off that body we all know you're hiding under there."

"There will be enough of that to go around tonight," she said back. "Wait—you can't leave yet," she said urgently, having apparently realized he was heading out.

Gavin frowned her way, but even as he started to reply,

two of his co-workers came out of the back with a small cake, sparklers erupting, and the number five drawn on in red atop the white icing.

Five years since the app's launch.

Claps sounded, and Gavin laughed sheepishly as a few of his friends and colleagues came from the back and congratulated him. He wavered through the throng, running his hand through his fluffy ginger hair and over his face, stopping to give them hugs and thanking them for their hard work, as he couldn't have done it without them. Until he reached Avril, and she handed him a gift that she'd stashed in the corner with the extra decor.

"You really didn't have to," Gavin told her as he opened the box. "What is it? Did you—" Red, fuzzy handcuffs fell into his hand, and he lifted a coy brow to her as whistles sounded from the rest of the crowd.

"Trying to tell me something, Av?" he asked.

"I think I speak for everyone when we say we hope you find someone to use them on tonight," she replied, and a few people clapped heartily while a couple of others grabbed him by the shoulders, shaking him in a ragging manner. Gavin grinned and stuffed the handcuffs in his back pocket just as his phone buzzed again.

Over a thousand invitations claimed.

"Alright, back to it—" He leaned over and kissed Avril on the cheek, then turned on his heel. "One hour until showtime."

One hour until Chloe could go home.

It was the amount of time Chloe had told her friend, Lana, that she would stay at this singles party Lana was so desperate to attend. It was being sponsored by the most popular dating app online right now, one that Lana was obsessed with and one that Chloe hardly had time for.

"It's not even a dating app," Chloe said as she looked through her closet.

"Sure it is," Lana argued, standing in front of the mirror and checking out her ass in the fitted red dress she was wearing.

"Name one actual date you've ever been on using that app," Chloe said.

"I went out with..." She paused, and Chloe laughed at her friend.

"Exactly."

But Lana ignored her. *"You can select what you're looking for,"* she argued. *"Marriage, one-night hook-up, casual, friends—"*

"Someone to murder you," Chloe muttered under her breath.

"Well," Lana turned and pulled a leather skirt from the closet, *"if that's what you're into,"* she winked.

Chloe adjusted the high-waisted, black leather mini-skirt Lana had chosen for her to wear as they waited in line. A rogue snowstorm had come in that day, and the chill of it had her pulling her long coat tighter around her body.

She was ready for a drink.

"Have your invitation?" Lana asked. "You have to RSVP to get in."

Chloe pulled her phone out, fingers nearly numb with the cold as she fumbled onto the app to accept the local invitation. She noted Lana's playful smile out of the corner of her eye.

"What?" Chloe asked.

"I knew you had the app," Lana teased.

They reached the door then, the bouncer giving them a quick, leering smile and once over before saying, "Enjoy, ladies," and letting them inside.

"Wait—I thought—"

Lana ignored Chloe and shrugged her leopard print coat off.

"You mean I didn't have to accept that stupid invitation?" Chloe asked.

"Of course not," Lana laughed. "I honestly just wanted to see if you had an account."

Chloe resisted her chuckle, shaking her head at her friend. "You're such a bitch," she declared.

"You love me," Lana shrugged.

Warmth finally hit Chloe's chilled cheeks as they moved further inside. The place was packed already—smells of alcohol and candy filling the air as though they were pumping it in. She could hardly hear the music due to the noises of people laughing and chatting, and drinks clanking. Lana found them a standing table, and Chloe eyed the drink menu, eager to get some alcohol in her shivering body.

There were six signature cocktails for the night, and Chloe laughed at the names for some.

"Love Potion Number Nine," she named off, smirking at her friend. "Because why wouldn't you have a drink named that at a Valentine's party?"

"These are fun," Lana said as she reached into the bowl of candy hearts and drew one out. "*CHOKE ME*," she read. "Well, at least they're direct."

Chloe took out a handful and laid them out on the table. "I like this one better," she said, pushing a heart in Lana's direction.

FUCK OFF, it read.

Lana laughed. "How many idiots do you think we can turn away tonight using only the candies?" And Chloe lit up at the idea.

"You're trying to get me to stay longer, aren't you?" Chloe asked.

"Obviously."

Chloe sat a heart on her own tongue, making sure Lana saw the word '*BLOCKED*' on it before curling it back into her mouth. Lana laughed as the waitress made her way through the crowd and spotted them. She was carrying a few of the night's cocktails, and Chloe chose a Scarlett Kiss while Lana chose a Love Potion.

"To finally getting you away from your computer," Lana teased, raising her glass.

Chloe laughed. "To this hour going by quickly so I can get out of these heels."

Lana arched a perfectly-trimmed, smug brow. "Someone will certainly be getting you out of those heels," she drawled. "Cheers to the one who does."

3

Everything was going according to plan.

Drinks were flowing. The music was a thudding white noise in the background to all the laughter and talking around the room. Gavin had chosen a seat at the far end of the bar so he could watch while he chatted with a few of his friends from work. He'd even found time to pull out the app and do a little dancing around with the profiles, nudge some people in the right direction for a strong connection, along with shifting a few he knew would be explosive in the end. He smirked proudly at himself for the brilliant toying as he watched some of the matches play out in front of him from his seat.

It was all perfect… a *normal* Valentine's night…

Until she walked in.

Fuck me, he thought as he noticed her.

Everything his friend, Zayn, was saying, muted. She was shrugging her black trench coat off, revealing the off-shoulder light pink sweater tucked into the wide belt over her leather mini-skirt, her full, pillowed breasts pushed up and exposed along the vee neckline. Her long legs were hidden beneath a sheer layer of black tights and thigh-high black heeled boots. It made him more curious about her, of whether she'd worn full tights or if they were connected to some slutty lingerie beneath.

He hoped it was the latter.

The fantasy of her in something strappy, perhaps sprawled out on the bed, her wrists locked together over her head with the his new handcuffs filled his mind. He already wanted to set those breasts free, feel how soft they would be in his mouth—

Shit, she'd barely been in the room three minutes and he was already plotting all the ways he could have her.

She laughed at something her friend said, absentmindedly pushing her long, silky black hair off her face as she reached for the drink menu. Her smoky makeup accented her warm ivory skin, highlighting her round, dark brown eyes. How fucking beautiful she would look on her knees... his hand threaded through her soft strands, those wide eyes looking up at him as she took his cock deep...

One of the neon red lights ricocheted off her friend's bouncing textured hair, caramel streaks in the tamed spirals, and bathed her light brown skin in its glare. They were looking at the candy hearts, and he couldn't fight his swallow as the girl he was admiring laid one on her tongue and rolled it back into her mouth.

Shit.

"Hey, Gav—" Zayn snapped his fingers in his face twice, and Gavin zipped out of the daze. Zayn was grinning at him, obvious he'd seen where his mind had wandered off to.

"She's cute," Zayn said, sipping his drink as he glanced her way.

"She is," Gavin agreed. "I don't remember seeing her on my list."

"Open party," Zayn shrugged. "Sure a few will slip in with friends."

Gavin did recognize her friend, had seen her profile before and the photos on it, and seen a few of the people she'd matched with…

Gavin took out his phone. He could have a little fun with this.

His friends continued to chat around him as he worked, sneaking glances up at her every now and then. He noticed a few guys coming up to chat and watched as the two women slid candy hearts in their directions. A few looked pissed off while others laughed, apparently intrigued by the game.

It had been a long time since he had genuinely lusted after anyone. Most that he'd found himself in bed with had been last-minute suggestions, mere glances exchanged that ended up with him taking them home and fucking in the back of his Jeep Wrangler.

This woman… He had a feeling he might have to do more than smile to get her attention.

He'd start with the basics.

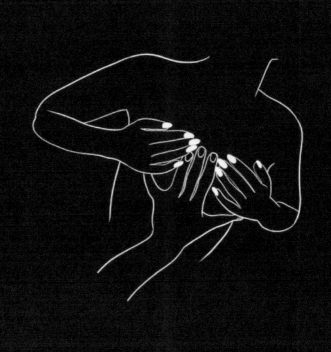

Chloe slid a candy heart reading 'THANK U, NEXT' toward the man that had approached to buy her a drink. It wasn't even that he wasn't good-looking. She was simply having entirely too much fun with the game she and Lana were playing. Even the onlookers were having fun with it once they found out what the pair were doing. A few had come up to them just to see what hearts they would give them.

For the first time in months, Chloe finally forgot about work. Her jaw unclenched, her eyes relaxed along with her shoulders. She kept her phone face down on the table, and every time she thought about checking her email, she reached for a candy heart or sip of her drink instead.

Shots of candy vodka were passed out from the waitress, and she and Lana cheers'd again before shooting them back.

"Have you seen him?" Lana nudged her.

"Seen who?" Chloe asked as she sorted through a few more of the candy hearts.

"The hot ginger in the corner that's been staring at you since we walked in," Lana said, drink hiding her lips.

Chloe looked up from the bowl, eyes narrowed at Lana's attempt at being secretive. "You realize you look even more suspicious doing that, right?" She turned back to the hearts and shook her head. "In the corner... let me guess. He's hidden in shadows with a very mysterious look about him."

"No, he's in full light," Lana countered. She hugged her drink closer, a leer in her gaze as she looked at him. "If you don't go talk to him, I will."

"Here you go," the waitress announced as she circled around, two more drinks on her tray—the pomegranate martinis that Chloe had been eager to try.

"Wait," Chloe interrupted. "We didn't order these."

"No," the waitress agreed, a smile splitting her red lips. "But he did," she added with a nod to the man at the end of the bar—the ginger she assumed Lana had been talking about.

At least Lana wasn't completely full of shit.

He was undoubtedly the sexiest thing she'd seen at that party.

Fluffy, dark ginger hair, strong brows, a pointed chin... He was structurally god-like, and she wondered what was wrong with him that he was at a singles party on Valentine's Day.

He was chatting with a few people who it looked like he knew. The deep dimple in his right cheek appeared with his crooked, flirtatious smile, that red scruff lining his jaw and upper lip at just the right length...

She took another sip of the sweet martini as she continued to look him over—noting the shadows of his strong shoulders creasing his cream-color sweater, his firm hand wrapping around his drink. He laughed and his buddy shook his shoulder a second, both looking to another friend who was animatedly saying something. Her gaze skated back to his face, noticing his pale skin now slightly illuminated by the flash of neon red from a spotlight swirling the room.

Her bottom lip drew behind her teeth as she suddenly imagined the scruff on his jaw scratching against her inner thighs, tickling her flesh, that lopsided grin against her—

Stop, she told herself.

But it had been entirely too long since she'd been thoroughly fucked, and she cursed herself for the imagery invading her mind. She took another sip of her drink, intent on turning back to Lana to ask her something, but whatever she meant to say wholly escaped her.

He was looking at her, and her heart skipped out of surprise.

His grin had faltered, soft almond-shaped eyes holding her own, his chin lifting just noticeably. The corner of his slightly agape mouth flinched almost like he would smirk, and he glanced down at his hands, tongue darting out over his lips before looking in her direction once more, and this time that smirk appeared just faintly on his parted mouth. The way his eyes washed over her made her feel as though he meant to claim her, and she couldn't control her shifting weight or her tightening thighs.

Shit, she was already tipsy and she was only on her third drink.

"Water," Chloe blurted before the waitress left the table. "Please."

The waitress snickered her way, but nodded before leaving them.

"Look at that," Lana drawled, toying with the straw in her drink that she was still nursing. "We have a winner."

"I bet he's a prick," Chloe said quickly, her face heating at the exchange as she turned back to the table. "Or doesn't know how to use his cock. Someone that pretty can't do it all."

"I have a feeling you're going to find out," Lana replied.

"Hi, ladies," a man announced as he and his friend approached. Handsome and with dark hair, Chloe wouldn't deny her attraction to them any more than she had the other men that had approached. The one that had spoken was eyeing Lana as though he knew her, and Chloe hid her grin behind her drink.

"It's Lana, right?" he asked.

Surprise lifted Lana's features. "Stalker status there, but yes, it is," she answered, intrigued.

The man held up his phone. "I saw where we matched, wanted to come say 'hi' instead of messaging since we were both here."

Lana frowned at the screen, much to Chloe's amusement. "I don't... I haven't been online since we got here." Lana fumbled to take her own phone out and check it. A couple of notifications were there that hadn't been before, and Lana tapped to find new matches.

"Wow, I must be drunker than I thought," she muttered before laying the phone face down and turning her attention to him. "Adam?"

Chloe tuned them out, quietly observing the rest of the crowd, wandering eyes going first to the spot that the handsome man had sat, and her heart fell when she saw he was no longer there.

Adam's friend tried talking to her, and because Lana was enjoying herself, Chloe didn't want to be totally rude to the guy, so she tried to listen while she looked around for her handsome stranger.

"Name is Chad," the friend said, and Chloe could feel him looking her wholly over, eyes lingering on her breasts. "It's always awkward, isn't it?"

Chloe's gaze darted to him, slightly annoyed he had introduced himself and went on about the conversation as though he'd no interest in her own name and was rather thoroughly intrigued by her breasts alone.

"What?" Chloe asked as she looked away to continue her search.

"Being the wingman," Chad explained before downing his

drink. "Third wheel. It makes me crazy."

Chloe's full attention diverted back. Another twinge of annoyance ticked inside her as her fingers coiled tightly around her martini. "You think I'm just here in case she decides she needs an excuse to leave early?" she snapped.

Chad watched her for a moment as his throat bobbed with a swallow of his drink. "No need to get an attitude, Princess," he said. "I'm here as his wingman."

"Princess…" She scoffed, hating when someone called her that in such a condescending manner. "I suppose you think that by default, we'll be sharing some sort of night together where you claim to please me?"

"I've been known to take one for the team," he said, eyes dancing deliberately over her once more. "Though with you, I think I might enjoy it."

"What makes you think I have any interest in you?"

He stepped closer. "You will."

"Will I?" She sat her drink on the table, hand resting on her hip as she held her head high in a challenging manner. "Do you also think I'll also enjoy the two pumps of your cock inside me before you get off," she snapped. "If you even make it there. From the looks of it, you're going to come in your pants staring at my breasts. Are you enjoying the view? They are directly in your face, after all."

Chad stared at her, the leer that had been in his eyes now vacant. "You should watch that attitude of yours," he said, his voice stiffening. "Try being less of a bitch."

She choked out a sarcastic laugh. "Poor thing, I bet you thought that was an insult," she said with a tilt of her head.

"Princess, taking you home tonight would be an insult to my reputation," he shot.

Chloe blinked, trying to keep calm. "Call me Princess again, and the ambulance will be the one taking you home," she said through a clenched smile.

"There you are—"

The new, rasping voice rose the hair on the back of her neck. A large hand slithered around her waist, soft lips and scruff brushing her skin as someone leaned down and kissed her temple. The smell of peppered musk entered her nostrils—a sweet, yet heated scent that she felt envelope her entire body like a warm, comforting blanket.

Chloe didn't have to look over to know that it was the sexy ginger stranger from the other side of the room that had joined her.

That damn smirk was staring at her when he practically skirted between her and Chad. "I've looked everywhere for you," he continued.

She reminded herself she shouldn't drink whiskey. It usually brought out her fight response.

She would stick to the vodka the rest of the night.

Sexy Ginger's gaze held her own as she inhaled deeply to calm herself, and she took a sip of her drink before giving him a teasing smile. "I told you what I was wearing," she finally replied, playing along and nearly jumping him for saving her from knocking Chad on his ass.

"You told me what you were wearing beneath it," he replied, crooking a flirtatious brow, those eyes shifting over her in a way that made her neck heat, her eyes darken. She resisted chuckling at the comment and the leering gaze he stared at her with.

"Not this ensemble," he finished.

Oh, he was good.

And she could tell by the mischievous glint in his eyes that he fucking knew it too.

Chad cleared his throat, and Hot as Sin pushed off the table, pretending to have just noticed him standing there.

"Oh, sorry, friend," Ginger said, giving Chad a clap on his shoulder. "I have blinders on when it comes to beautiful women. I didn't notice you there."

Chad's jaw clenched, and Chloe noticed Sexy Ginger's fingers gripping tighter and tighter around Chad's shoulder, almost like a warning. She could see Chad's expression faltering, pain stretching across his features as Ginger sunk his fingers deep into Chad's clavicle.

"I was just—"

"Finding someone else to bother?" Sexy Ginger suggested, his expression growing stern.

Chloe shifted at the demand and brazen nature of the act, hating herself for how much it was turning her on.

Chad's hand clenched so tightly around his glass that Chloe thought it might break. "I was just going to get a drink for my friend," Chad said through unmoving teeth.

Sexy released Chad's shoulder slowly, and then he did something that made Chloe's eyes widen.

He mockingly tapped Chad's cheek twice, and said, "Good boy," in a threateningly deep, sardonic tone that even sent a warning pulse all the way to *Chloe's* core.

Seeming to think the exchange was over, Sexy Ginger turned his attention back to Chloe with a sigh and lift of that smirk on his lips… smiling as though he had successfully rid them of a pest. But Chloe saw Chad's glaring face turn a deep shade of carmine. He set his drink on the table, his fists curling, and she realized the idiot was about to come at them.

Chloe stepped forward and threw her full drink in Chad's face before he could make his move.

Whistles sounded around, a few 'Ooo's' followed with laughter. Chad sputtered and wiped his eyes of the stinging alcohol, and Chloe slammed her empty glass on the table.

"If you're going to hit someone, don't be a fucking coward and do it while their back is turned," she snapped.

"What—*the fuck happened, bro?*"

Adam pushed between her and Sexy Ginger just as Lana

grabbed Chloe's arm.

"Damn, Clo," Lana chuckled. "Hate to know what got that reaction. I need to bring you out more often. You're living all my dreams tonight."

A waitress came by then and pulled a rag from her apron. She shook it out and handed it to Chad, and without saying a word to the idiot, she turned to Chloe.

"New drink?" she asked, apparently amused by the scuffle.

"Please," Chloe replied.

Sexy Ginger was staring down at Chloe, a smile on his lips, his brows slightly narrowed as though he were still processing what had just happened.

"Now we're even," Chloe said, smirking up at him.

"I misread the room," he said, hand clenching his chest. "Here I thought you were a damsel in need of saving. Turns out you're the fucking knight."

The waitress handed him a rag to wipe his face as some had managed to splatter in his direction, and he gave her a nod. "Thank you, Wendy."

"No problem, Gav," she replied. "Another?"

"I think so," he said slowly, watching Chloe again with an intrigued stare.

But Chloe's attention moved to Adam and Chad, who were still cleaning up, cursing the girls and glowering at the onlookers who continued to laugh and snicker behind their backs.

"Isn't it always the thing with men?" Chloe mused, lashes lifting to her sexy stranger along with her chin. "Showing off that testosterone and manly urge to claim and fight."

That damn dimple appeared on the right side of his angled grin as he reached into the bowl of candy hearts and proceeded to lay a few out on their table.

YOU'RE MINE

BE MINE
R U MINE
I'M YOURS
U R MINE

"Are you saying I should trash these, then, so they don't make their way into our game later?" he asked.

She could practically feel her eyes dilating at the mention of a game and naughty candy hearts. "I've never played that game."

"Don't worry. I'll teach you the rules," he said.

"Never really been a fan of those. I like to make my own."

He scoffed, gaze traveling over her as he sucked his lip behind his teeth, obvious he was charmed by her banter and perhaps debating on his next move.

"Gavin," he introduced himself.

There was a name she could hear herself screaming later.

"Gavin..." she said, letting his name stick and tattoo on her tongue like a song she couldn't get out of her head. "I'm Chloe," she told him. "This is my friend, Lana."

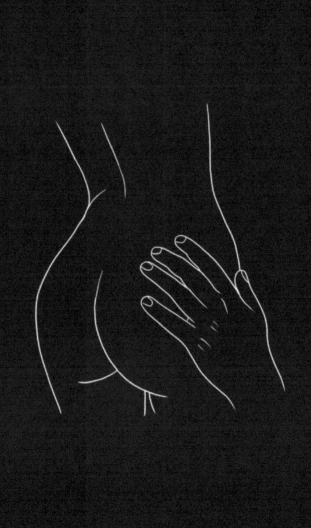

Chloe.

Oh, he couldn't wait to say that name later. Taste that name. Taste *her*.

It wasn't exactly how he'd anticipated his first meeting with her, but his heart was fluttering after seeing her throw her drink in that guy's face.

He had nearly kissed her right then.

And the way she was grinning at him had his heartbeat picking up.

"You're not a serial killer, are you, Gavin?" her friend, Lana, interjected herself into the conversation as she leaned her elbows on the table, her slight cleavage pushing up between her arms. "—Actually, if you are, I hope she's the one who makes you change your ways. Helps you see the light." Lana gave him a wink, and he couldn't help his amused huff.

"And that's *good-by*e, Lana," Chloe said with a full, mocking smile. "Don't you have someone else to talk to?" she added with a nod to the man that had just sat his drink down on the table behind her. Lana grinned around the straw in her mouth, and she shifted her attention to her new friend.

Chloe shook her head as she turned back to Gavin, and her gaze seemed to pour through him a moment before she spoke.

"You're not a serial killer, are you?" she asked as the waitress sat their drinks down.

"What if I told you I was Cupid?" he asked, only half-teasing.

"Then I would say you're worse than a serial killer," she replied. "You make people fall in love."

"Love is death?"

"Love is unrealistic and tragic," she answered. "No matter how much you love someone or something, death eventually take it away."

"Everyone loves something," he countered. "Shouldn't love be part of life's enjoyment? Otherwise what's the point?"

She seemed to consider it, her short, square black nails tapping on the martini glass. "If you are Cupid, what are you doing here? Shouldn't you be flying around, shooting arrows in people's asses?"

He chuckled softly, resisting telling her that he was fully capable of doing that with his phone now. "Taking the night off," he answered.

"Oh? Isn't this a popular night?"

"It's a bit cliche to fall in love on Valentine's Day, don't you think?" he bantered. "Besides, I've found something much more intriguing to spend my night with."

"What's that?" And the way her eyes dilated made a smile lift the corner of his mouth.

"You."

She stared at him a moment, lips twisting in amusement, a soft glisten rising in her eyes like she was holding in laughter. "Did you steal that from a romance novel?" she asked.

"Heard one of the other idiots at the end of the bar say it," he replied. "Thought I would see if it worked."

"Did it work for him?"

"It did not."

"Why would you think it would work on me, then?"

"You look like you read romance novels," he said, his smirk widening. "I thought the line might spark your curiosity. Make you feel like you were in one. The truly dirty kind, of course."

"Sorry, you're not really my type in that genre," she said as she sat down her glass.

"What's your type?"

Her chin lifted, and the mockery playing in her round brown eyes made him want to pull her flush and dip his hand beneath that skirt to see how wet she was from the last fifteen minutes of excitement.

"Minotaurs," she answered.

Gods, she was fucking cute.

He settled his elbow against the wood, eyeing the smug look on her face. He was sure she thought that word would send him running for the hills. She hadn't stopped smiling since he'd come over, her confidence radiating with every rise and fall of her breasts. And the way those eyes glittered up at him had him wild for her.

"Here I thought you looked more like the faerie erotica type," he teased, voice dropping.

She paused for a moment, evident that she was trying to keep herself from grinning outright as she twisted her red-stained lips, pulling her cheeks in and biting. He stifled a groan as he imagined how those lips would pucker and plump around his cock, how that scarlet color would smear so beautifully around her mouth…

"You seem to know a lot about fantasy romance," she said, drawing him out of the trance.

"I'm Cupid," he shrugged. "It's part of my job to know these things."

There was a brief second when it looked like she was genuinely considering the possibility. Her bright eyes squinted slightly, nails strumming on her glass again.

"Okay, *Cupid*," she said, saying his name like it was a joke. "Is that—"

A drunk man cut between them then, laughing as one of his friends had pushed him. Chloe jolted back, hugging her drink to her, but the new man seemed dazed and confused when he looked up and found her staring.

"I've fallen and found an angel," the man said.

Gavin couldn't keep his soft laughter down. Chloe caught his eye as she rolled her own, and Gavin reached into the bowl of candy hearts.

One of the friends shook the drunk man's shoulders as Gavin stepped out from behind them. The three men were still gathering their wits, not paying attention to the pair, and Gavin took the opportunity to move to Chloe's side.

Brushing halfway in front of her, he held up the candy heart he'd chosen, letting her see it briefly and gauging the look in her eyes before bending to whisper, "Open wide," into her hair, his finger delicately tugging her chin.

Pure lust rose in those shimmering eyes... lust that he intended to take advantage of in every way these naughty candy hearts told him to later, and her lips parted just so. He held her gaze hostage as he placed the heart on her tongue, and for a moment, it was all he could do to hold himself back from moving further... from skimming his thumb on her pouting red lip, grazing his finger along her highlighted cheek, or curling his hand in her silky hair...

That white candy heart on her tongue was a siren's song to his crazed, immortal soul—calling him out on his insatiable desire for this woman... *this* woman...

He needed to consume her.

To touch her.

Taste her.

Feel her.

A whisper of his touch against her throat was the last thing he left her with before making his way back across the room.

The candy heart seemed to burn on her tongue. His touch was a brand she couldn't get out of her head. She could still feel his fingers on her chin, brushing her throat, her mind remaining in a stupor over the way his gruff whisper had made the hair on her neck rise…

Chloe was still staring off into space, reliving the last few seconds, her entire neck and face heated, when Lana pushed up behind her.

"That was *hot*," Lana said in a low tone, leaning eagerly on her elbows beside her. "God, that was hot. What did the heart say?"

Chloe crushed the heart between her teeth and met Lana's eyes. "Be mine," she answered.

Lana slumped as though the words had made her weak. "Fuck off, Clo," she said. "You go out one night and you find the hottest thing that's also charming and not a complete dick. Where is this luck of mine?"

One of the men that had come to join their table cleared his throat, and Lana stared at him.

"Too eager." She slid over a candy that read *BOI BYE* in his direction, but all he did was laugh.

Chloe sipped her water as Lana and the new man, David, began bantering back and forth. His friend, Devon, tried chatting with Chloe, but it was all Chloe could do not to try and find Gavin in the crowd.

Chloe's one-hour timer went off, and Lana raised a brow in her direction.

And she hated admitting that she wanted to stay longer.

However, she couldn't stop thinking about him.

Lana's face lit up as she watched Chloe hit the 'dismiss' button, and then she threw her hands in the air with a loud cheer—going so far as to flag down the waitress for another round of candy shots.

Chloe shot back the liquid while flipping Lana off.

No matter how intriguing the conversation might have been with Lana and the three men laughing with them, Chloe couldn't stop her wandering eyes.

It was almost as though his entire presence had been a fantasy.

Someone bumped into Chloe a few minutes later, a hand sliding softly on her waist, and she swore she felt a finger dig into her belt. But the touch was gone within a second, and the person had fluttered back into the crowd by the time she managed to turn around.

There was something pressed beneath her belt.

She dug into it, and she had to bite her lips together upon seeing the candy heart.

HEY SEXY

She tried searching around her without making it obvious, eventually finding Gavin's handsome face in the crowd, and she popped the candy into her mouth, deliberately rolling it back on her tongue, when she did.

Fuck, he was cute.

That damn dimple appeared when he smiled crookedly at her, one hand shoving in his pockets as he turned back and pretended to laugh with his friends. He'd pushed the sleeves of his snug-fitting cream sweater up, revealing a few tattoos on those forearms. Forearms that she wanted to see extended from her neck as he wrapped those long fingers around her throat. She eyed the firm grip he held on his drink, warmth pooling between her thighs at the vision of that grip on her ass or entwined in her hair.

A popular song came on the jukebox, and the entire bar erupted in cheers. Chloe pulled herself out of the trance as Lana jumped up and down at her side, her arm punching the air. Lana grabbed one of the guys they were chatting with and dragged him close to her, making Chloe laugh out loud as she tried to dance with him. But the man, David, kept up with her, and Chloe found herself standing back and nursing her cocktail as she watched.

When she looked over for Gavin, he was gone.

"Who knew this song could cause such a *distraction*."

Heat stretched from her ears down her spine and between her legs at the sound of Gavin's voice. She hugged her arms tighter as she continued to watch Lana. David twirled Lana, making her hair bounce, and Lana's smile became so bright that it was like the entire room was suddenly her own stage.

Chloe leaned a little closer to Gavin, their arms brushing. "It would be a perfect move of the hero in a romance novel to put this song on so that everyone was looking the other way just so he could swoon the heroine off her feet," she said before pivoting to face him.

"I agree," he said. "The hero would probably ask her to dance with him. Maybe tell her how beautiful she looked or how he admired her outfit."

"He'd be a gentleman about it, too," she added. "Sing a little to her. Offer to buy her another drink. Of course, he would keep his hands to himself and not do anything... *inappropriate*."

"Your hero sounds like an idiot," Gavin bantered.

Chloe resisted her laugh as she swirled her drink. "You

didn't happen to turn on this song, did you?"

Gavin's deep chuckle and devious smirk made her shift. He took her drink from her hand and sat both their glasses on the table behind her. Chloe's breath hitched as he pressed his hands into the edge of the table on either side of her, enclosing the gap so that their bodies were nearly flush. With her heels, he was only a few inches taller. His warmth blanketed over her as she lifted her lashes, watching his blown pupils travel over her face, eventually landing on her own, and she found herself unable to look away.

"Sweet girl, I'm not your hero," he rasped. "I'm the god of lust... *desire*... I'm the shadow you see in the dark when you think someone is watching you touch yourself, the blank face you see when you stare at the walls and imagine someone between your thighs. I'm the god you pray to when your thighs shake and your breaths cease... I'm *every* wicked fantasy you've ever had."

"All of them?" she managed, her thighs squeezing at the restless ache suddenly present between them.

His chest pressed to hers, his head bent lower, and Chloe found herself staring at his lips, her hands slightly grasping at his sweater. The soft thread burned beneath her fingertips as she felt his next words hit her lips.

"Be mine tonight, and I'll show you."

The room erupted with more cheers. The song finished, and Gavin took a step back. That smile grew again as the darkness lifted from his green eyes. Lana's laughter pulled Chloe out of her daze as she nearly fell into the table, David holding her arms and smiling with her.

And when Chloe turned to say something to Gavin, he was gone.

She wished he would stop disappearing like that.

But on the table beside her drink was another heart.
R U WET

She wanted him to find out for himself.

She could still smell his cologne lingering in the air. Still feel his breath on her lips as he spoke those words. She turned around, head on a swivel looking for his hair, and she spotted him back with the friend he'd been chatting with most of the night.

Chloe grabbed one of the hearts and made her way across the room, making sure to stay out of his sightline as she maneuvered through the crowd. When she reached him, she slid her hand in his back pocket, dropped the heart in securely, and then pushed past him toward the bathroom.

The white stalls were a hum of noise in comparison to the rowdy bar.

Chloe paused at the first sink and pressed her hands into the porcelain. Thank fuck she'd been nursing that last martini and switching with water. There were a few girls in the stalls puking, and she was glad that wasn't her.

Her gaze met her own in the mirror.

Chloe worked fast to revive her face and hair, reapplying the faint dark red stain she'd been wearing on her lips, now faded slightly from the drinking. Perking her girls up and adjusting the wide belt on her waist, checking out her ass in the long mirror and her thigh-high boots.

I'd fuck you, she could hear Lana telling her earlier when she'd picked out the outfit.

"You look hot, girl," a woman, much drunker than her, said from the sinks.

She loved the camaraderie of drunken women in bathrooms.

"Thank you," Chloe said as she adjusted her belt again. "So do you," she smiled at her new friend.

One last look over herself, and she exited the bathroom.

Outside the bathroom was a neon red sign with hearts on the wall, the only light source in the darkened hall. Chloe's eyes immediately searched the more lit-up bar room as she walked, wondering if Gavin had felt her reaching into his pocket. She was hoping he'd read that heart and wanted to find her.

A hand grabbed and pulled her backward, pushing her back into the wall. Her heart skipped as a toned body pressed flush to her own. The rich smell of Gavin's cologne hit her as his shadow consumed her, leaving only that red light to highlight the strongest parts of his features. He was so close that he was pressing into her in just the right places.

Fuck, he smelled good.

Her chest rose jaggedly against him, thigh coming between his, and she rolled her body against his. "Is this how you normally get women into your bed?" she breathed, chin craning upward to expose her neck. "Cornering them beneath the red lights… whispering dangerous quotes in their ears—" her back arched, pressing herself more into him, and she let her fingers crawl one at a time up his shirt. "—*teasing* what you're capable of?"

She could see the hunger shadowed in his eyes, and the right corner of his lips flinched.

"Teasing? Is that why you put this in my pocket?" He closed his mouth, tongue working, and when he opened his mouth again, the pink candy heart that read '*TEASE ME*' was gripped between his front teeth.

Her lips threatened to lift as her gaze darted from his eyes to that heart, debating whether to take it out of his mouth or remove herself from beneath him… to make him watch her walk away as he had done to her.

She reached around his hips, intent on pulling him closer to her, and she felt something in the opposite back pocket from what she'd had her hand in earlier. But what she grabbed, she didn't expect.

Fuzzy red handcuffs.

Her brow elevated as she pulled them out, and she dangled them mockingly in front of his face, catching his chuckle as he popped the candy heart back into his mouth. The dangerous look in his eyes made her stomach knot. All she could see was herself stretched out on the bed, feeling the soft fur on the cuffs around her wrists, his scruff on her thighs...

"Something you're planning?" she asked.

He shifted his weight, head leaning closer. "*Every* fantasy," he promised. "You just have to be mine tonight."

She considered it, holding those cuffs as she slithered her hands up his chest, her knee bending, high heel pressing into the wall. His hands wrapped her waist, slightly squeezing the top of her ass as their hips pressed flush together. He was close... *so* close she could almost taste him. His open mouth hovering in front of hers... One breath and she would be giving in, knowing the moment their lips met that this was over.

She would be his.

She pushed on his chest, and Gavin stumbled off balance as he released her. That lopsided smirk dared to dance on his lips and in his eyes, and she felt her lips twist teasingly as she turned on her heel back to the party.

But not before flicking another candy heart his way.

BITE ME

She was going to be the death of him.

He was sure of it.

He'd lived centuries, delved in desires and toyed with people's emotions for all of them. But this girl... He had to have her. And he would use none of his godly tricks to get her. She would be his of her own accord.

And damn, did he love the game they were playing.

She had stuck her tongue out and made a face at him as she'd flicked the heart his way, then turned, her hips swaying, making sure to step one long leg in front of the other. A deliberate tease he knew she was reveling in. Her sweater had even fallen a little more off her shoulder. And when she reached her friend, she took a long drink of water and pushed her hair to one side, exposing the neck he wanted to kiss and suck and choke.

Gavin stayed by the bar.

"Why are you still here?" He heard Avril saying as she approached him. "What—I thought you'd left with that pretty girl already," she added. Her hand lifted to the bartender for another drink, and she leaned on the bar at his side.

Gavin grinned in that devious way, his eyes only briefly

moving away from Chloe to Avril. "Games," he told her as he took a swig of his drink.

"I'm too old for games," she grunted, and Gavin laughed. "Much rather be direct."

He reached over the bar for a clean bag of naughty candy hearts that they'd had made as favors. "Games are fun, Av…" he said as he shoved it in his back pocket—

Realizing Chloe had kept the handcuffs.

He laughed under his breath and shook his head at the floor again.

"What's so funny?" Avril asked.

"She kept the fucking handcuffs," he said, eyes landing on Chloe.

A quiet laugh escaped Avril, and she touched his arm as she made to walk away. "Don't let that one go."

It was twice within the next half hour that he brushed by her side, never stopping, and he left a heart in her belt each time. And each time, she watched him with baited eyes, without a single word. But he always felt her lean into his touch, saw her chest heave when approached, like her body was responding to his simply being near her.

The third time he started to go by her, she wasn't there, and he ended up circling the entire room and checking his phone before going back to the bar, his heart knotting as he thought perhaps she had left.

He had screwed up, waited too long. She'd slipped through his grasp.

Until he saw her sitting in the seat he'd been occupying most of the night, fingers steepled beneath her chin as she watched him come near her, a knowing smirk on those pouting lips.

He slowed in his approach, his chin lifting at her smug figure as a flutter filled his stomach.

"You know, for a minute, I thought maybe you were

scouting the floor for another woman to bother," she said as she toyed with the straw in her drink. "Then I realized you were looking for me."

Gavin sat his glass on the bar. "I believe you have something of mine."

"Took it for insurance."

"What for?"

"Making sure you didn't decide to leave without me."

And his cock twitched at the hunger in her eyes.

She uncrossed her legs and crossed them back, *slowly*, the edge of her skirt hiking just enough that he could see it was, in fact, stockings on her legs instead of tights. A lust-filled restriction sounded in the back of his throat at the sight of the clips attaching them to whatever slutty lingerie she wore beneath those damn clothes. He stepped closer, needing her to know what she was doing to him.

"Sweet girl..." He dared to brush his knuckles on that exposed flesh... dared to flick his finger beneath the strap and give it a gentle tug. Her eyes held his, and he said in a throaty rasp, "I don't plan on leaving here without you."

Her breath visibly caught as his hand moved higher, never losing her stare. He delicately caressed her skin, savoring the softness beneath his fingers, and as his fingers hit the bend of her hip, he reached into his back pocket.

"Put these in your bag with the handcuffs," he told her.

She eyed the red drawstring baggie, and when she opened it, he watched delight lift on every inch of her face. "What are these for?"

His lips tugged upwards, and he leaned closer to her, turning so that both his hands were on her thighs. "I plan on doing everything that these hearts say. Striping you. Biting you. Sucking you. All of them... One at a time... One command after the other... Over and over until you beg me to stop," he said in her ear. "And when you do, I'll—"

"Let me guess," she interjected. "You'll make me see God?"

"Baby, tonight, I am your god," he said, squeezing her flesh. "And you're the woman that's going to bring Eros to his knees."

Her tongue darted out over her lips, and he resisted capturing it with his teeth. "I like the sound of that," she said.

He scoffed. "I thought you might."

Her neck extended in his direction, their noses nearly brushing, but didn't let her get any closer. A heavy sigh left him as he forced himself to straighten over her, still stroking her thighs. "I just need one thing from you," he said.

"What's that?"

"Say you're mine."

He was ready to beg for her.

He didn't know how much more of the dance he could take.

He wanted to touch her everywhere. Taste her in every way. Soak her up as she spilled on his tongue and cried out his name. He needed to feel her body around his own. Just the warmth of her flesh had him on edge. It was taking everything in him not to press further, to uncross her legs so he could stand between them or whisper his hand across the nipples he knew were hardened beneath her fucking bra.

Chloe's smile widened. She shifted, and as her feet hit the ground, he wrapped his arm around her waist. He wanted her answer. He wanted *her*. Her breasts brushed against his chest, and he squeezed her waist as she trickled her fingers over his firm forearm, his hair rising with her every touch.

"Cherry vodka," the bartender announced as she set a drink in front of them and left with two slaps to the bar top.

Chloe broke her daze with Gavin to reach for the drink, but he couldn't look away. And when she drew the juicy cherry down the toothpick, his insides lit on fire at the sight of her pressing it to her puckered lips, letting it sit for a moment before pulling it back and crushing it in her teeth.

He almost fell to his knees at the red liquid dripping from the corner of her mouth, and he contained his urge to lick it off her face. She caught the drip with her tongue, her lashes lifting and hitting her eyelids when she smiled.

Gods, that fucking smile.

That fucking… *her*.

She knew she was making him crazy, and fuck… he *loved* it.

"Thanks for the drink," was all she said before hugging that glass to her chest and pushing past him, back to the table with Lana.

Gavin scoffed aloud, head sinking to his chest like he'd just been shot down.

"Bad luck tonight?" the bartender teased as she dried off a glass.

"I think she's testing to see how long it'll take me to break," Gavin said.

The bartender grinned. "How's that going for you?"

"I'm fucking shattered," Gavin admitted in an amused breath.

The bartender laughed, her short blue curls bouncing when she threw her head back. "It's Valentine's Day, Cupid," she jested. "Shouldn't the god of desire himself get the girl?"

A joke to his job title, he knew, but it filled his chest with pride nonetheless. His gaze flickered back to Chloe, and he asked the bartender to put both their tabs on his before he made his final descent into her magnetic abyss.

Lana was laughing at a joke when Gavin approached their table again, so he snuck in behind Chloe while she was distracted. He wrapped his hands around Chloe's waist and squeezed her soft flesh. She seemed to know it was him without looking, for she leaned back into him, and her hand grazed over his.

"Hello, Cupid," she said as he bent down to her ear.

"You know… all this begging you're making me do…" he rasped into her hair, "I might have to punish you for it later," he whispered. "You've been a *very* bad girl, teasing me all night."

Her head moved sideways just so, and he could see a smile lift at the corner of her lips. "Tell me how you'll punish me," she said in a voice only he could hear.

"Over my knees," he said, clutching her waist. "And you'll only be wearing those fluffy handcuffs."

Her ass shifted back into him, making his cock twitch at the feeling of that pressure. "Promise?" she asked.

He held her hip firm as he pressed into her, and his chuckle filled her ear as he said in a throaty breath, "Sweet girl… I *swear* it."

A soft laugh escaped her. She turned to her right, reaching into the candy dish on the bar top. He watched as she chose one of the candy hearts, and as she circled into him, she placed it on her tongue.

I'M YOURS

Every muscle in his body snapped to attention. But, he held his composure, and he watched her a quiet second before reaching into the bowl himself to look for a particular heart he intended to keep plenty of on hand for the rest of the night.

And, when he found it, he held her gaze, and he placed the candy on his tongue.

GOOD GIRL

She looked like the heart had triggered her to the very depths of her soul. Her chest visibly caved with her exhale, brown eyes dancing from his own to his lips. And just as he started to curl the candy back into his mouth, she grabbed him by his sweater, and her open mouth crashed into his.

She didn't know what had come over her. Why seeing that particular heart on his tongue had sent her entire body into overdrive.

But it did.

Fuck, it did.

His hands wrapped her waist, her neck. He was squeezing her flesh, his tongue sweeping against hers, fingers tugging gently at the roots of her hair. Those lips... those hands... she couldn't wait to have them on every inch of her. Heat pooled between her legs, and her heart thudded in her ears. A sick adrenaline shivered over her, making her forget that they were in the middle of a crowded bar, until he slowed his eagerness, and he pulled back.

Breaths short, his forehead rested against hers, digits still clamped on her waist. She was practically on fire from that kiss. Shit, that kiss had her spinning.

She needed more.

Her clenched fists tightened on his sweater again, and she leaned up, licking his open mouth, making him lean in again to kiss her, but she swayed back.

"My place."

Lana barely did more than give Chloe a kiss on her cheek and tell her to be safe—reminding her to use protection,

43

which Chloe swore she was up to date on—as Gavin left her to get his coat from the seat he'd been in before. Chloe shot back another swig of her drink, making a face at the sting of the last drops on her tongue. She no sooner had thrown her coat over her arm before a hand grabbed her waist and whirled her around. Gavin hauled her flush, his lips pressing against hers in a claiming kiss that limped her knees.

That dangerous, crooked smirk flashed down at her when he let her go, only to lean his lips into her hair and whisper, "Walk us to my Jeep. Give me a preview of that ass swaying like it'll do on my lap later."

She forgot how cold it was outside.

The chilled air hit her cheeks the moment they exited the packed bar. Sounds muted in the absence of the music and laughter, replaced with the noise of cars passing by. She tugged on Gavin's hand and looked back at him, noticing how he was watching her every movement, that dilation filling his eyes like he could consume her soul if he tried. Her heart throbbed in her ears every time he squeezed her fingers. She had to stop herself from nearly skipping to the black Jeep Wrangler parked beneath a street lamp.

The Jeep's lights flickered when he unlocked the doors, and with one glance over her shoulder at his darkened eyes, she let his hand go and reached for the handle. It opened—

Gavin crashed into her back, the door snapping close as he trapped her between his heated body and the cold metal. Chloe groaned at the strength of him over her, his nose in her hair, hands on her hips and fisting her skirt in his grasp. She arched back into him, mouth agape as his lips pressed to her neck, and she moved her ass against his pelvis just as he raised her skirt a fraction—only enough that the bare part of her thighs above her stockings was exposed. A shiver washed over her as the wind hit her skin, but it didn't pull her from the daze. Her arm snaked behind his head, body rocking against his, forgetting that they were on the street in front of everyone.

"Do you want it right here," he asked in a breath, his hardening length pressing into her backside. His touch traveled from her hips to her front, one finger whispering over the tiny lace thong she wore, making her flinch.

"Should I bend you over the front of my car?" he whispered in her hair. "Would you like everyone to watch?"

His tease made her eyes roll, her mouth sag. "Yes," she answered.

His finger dipped beneath the lace, and he chuckled into her neck as that pad grazed her throbbing clit. "You're so wet for me," he said with a groan. "I could slide inside you so easily... Hold my hand over your mouth... Tease you until tears fall down your beautiful cheeks, and you beg for more..." His rasp shivered over her body, and she couldn't stop her hips from moving against his finger. "Will you beg for me tonight, baby?"

Her heated breath fogged the window, body melting into his embrace, but he had other plans. He grabbed her waist and flipped her around. She jolted into the car door. He pinned her wrists by her head, and his lips met hers. Biting and eager. She could feel his stiffness against her abdomen, and she pushed her hips towards him, bringing her bent leg up. He let go of her left wrist, hand wrapping beneath her thigh and moving it higher on his waist. And when he released her other wrist, allowing her to hold her hands on his cheeks, she felt him squeeze her ass so hard that she moaned into his mouth.

She'd just pulled back when she felt his touch on her jaw, thumb stroking her lip. "Once you get in this car... you're all mine."

She breezed his stomach with her fingers, allowing them beneath the shirt so she could feel the warmth of his skin, feel his muscles constricting and flinching at her touch. And as her nails scratched just delicately over his flesh, she tilted her head back and wrapped her lips around his thumb.

His chest collapsed heavily as she sucked his finger, and then she whispered, "Show me your shadow in the dark... *Cupid.*"

She thought his gaze had held licentious desire and wickedness in them before... but at the very mention of that name, she swore all green evacuated beneath his widened pupils, and he laughed.

The man *laughed*.

It was a laugh that cradled her bones in a sudden craving for every part of him. A laugh that heated and curled her blood, quickened her heart and called to the deepest parts of her soul. She had wanted him before... but now...

Now, she would do everything to have him.

"Oh, sweet girl—"

His hand slid down her neck and tightened on her throat, making her breath hitch, her heart stumble, as he hovered over her, the dimple shining beneath his scruff.

"—You're going to regret calling me that."

Fuck, he was hot.

The kiss he pressed to her lips was fleeting, and he held her face in his hand as he said, "Put your address in," before opening the door for her. He was still watching her as she crawled in, a seriousness taking over his eyes, his mouth sagging with every labored breath, and he pinched her ass before winking and closing the door.

The click of that door sent a pulse through her. Adrenaline and desire mingled and entwined through her veins like they were carrying poison straight to her staggering heart. She was almost giddy with want for this man.

She sat up to her knees in the seat and started punching in her address on the GPS screen once he'd entered the driver's seat and turned over the engine. Rock music blared in the speakers, and neither bothered turning it down. His seatbelt clicked. He put the car in drive, and as he pulled out into traffic, a sharp ache of excitement surged through her stomach. Her body threw back into the seat at his acceleration. An unexpected laugh left her lips, and Gavin just smirked at her in response.

The bass vibrated the entire car as he swerved through downtown. Every flashing red light and headlight passing by reflecting off his features had her eager body restless. She pushed back up to her knees and leaned over in his direction, wanting to tease him as he'd been teasing her. He opened up to her without hesitation, and as he wrapped his right hand around her waist, she bent over the console.

His skin tasted like he smelled, like candy and musk and dangerous peppered vanilla spice. He tasted like dessert, and she wanted to know if he tasted that way everywhere. She reached to his pants, a moan escaping her when she felt his cock stiffening beneath her hand.

And when they slowed to a stoplight, he took both hands off the wheel to wrap around her face and kiss her hard. Desperately, like this was his last night on earth. She sucked his tongue as she pulled back, their eyes meeting beneath a sliver of the red glare from the light, and she whispered, "Slide back," before kissing him again.

He groaned in her mouth, but she felt the seat jerk as he shifted.

A horn blew.

Chloe looked up for the controls, rolled back the soft-top just enough to get her hand through, and she flipped off the person behind them as Gavin jammed on the accelerator. She threw back in the seat with another laugh, hanging onto his arm to keep herself steady, and she met his sideways smile.

"So, *Cupid*…" she said, shifting back up to his side. She

kissed his scruff-covered cheek, unbuttoning his pants as he slipped that right arm back around her waist. She pulled his length from the slit in his boxer briefs, nearly salivating at the size and length of him. Her hand wrapped firmly around his tip, and she heard him groan at the sensation.

"You like that?" she whispered as she watched his eyes flutter. His answer came in another groan as she continued to stroke him, relishing that power over him, knowing one slip could have them crashing into another vehicle.

It was the thrill of being exposed that she wanted then. Thrill that she hadn't felt in a long time. He made her feel invincible and sexy, desired and powerful. It was hot, and she was soaking from the intensity of him.

She settled her knees, arched her back, and lifted her ass high in the air as she bent down to his lap. And when her lips wrapped around his tip, he cursed her name.

"Fuck yes," he whispered as he fisted the bottom of her skirt high, exposing her thong and the straps over her bare ass that attached to her stockings. He massaged her ass, smacking it hard, and she moaned on his cock.

"Just like that," he uttered as he smacked her ass again. "Gods, yes."

The force of his spank had her soaking more than she already was. She lowered her mouth, stretching over his girth, slowly tonguing that taut cock, and moving her backside as he toyed with the thong between her cheeks.

His dick hit the back of her throat. Again and again. And the further she took him into oblivion, the further he reached over around her ass. Curling those fingers and grazing her entrances, cursing when he felt her wetness. But as he seemed to think about teasing her, she took him all the way in again, gagging on his thickness taking up and swelling down her throat, and his hand moved from her ass to the back of her head.

"Fuck, baby." His voice was hardly more audible than a whisper as his hips moved in her direction. His fingers wrapped in her hair, his legs spreading wider to adjust himself. "You want my cock deeper, sweet girl?" he asked as they slowed for another stoplight.

She pulled back slowly, head tilting as she tongued his tip. "Yes," she answered.

"You like showing off that pussy in the dark, don't you?" he asked. "Does it make you wetter? Knowing how many people are salivating at that ass in the window? At how many people have been staring and watching you suck my dick at these stoplights?"

She groaned around his cock at the thought as she started sucking on him again. Thankfully, the window was at least a little tinted, so her ass wasn't totally out... However, she couldn't deny that she liked the idea that people could see her silhouette like this. She'd never really been a public play person, but this... *this* was intoxicating. She could have done this all night—fucked him with the roof totally off, not just this soft-top rolled back. She could have watched people get off at the sight of her riding him, put on a show for the rest of this fucking town.

The fantasy of fucking him like that made her hum on his length and take him deeper. Knowing how the stop lights and street lamps would cascade on them and reflect off the drops of water and puddles left behind by the snow... How that cold, misty air would tease her skin... how his fingers would dig into her ass—

His middle finger dipped inside her, and he chuckled deeply, cock twitching in her mouth. "Gods, that *is* making you wetter. Do you think you deserve to choke on my cock for that?"

Her answer hummed around his length, and she felt the seat move as his head hit the headrest, his hand tightening in her hair again. The grip sent a shiver over her skin—the tightness and release. The slow help and guide of his grasp begged her to take him deeper, to salivate around his length and choke when he held her there too long.

And she did.

She let him push her. She let him choke her. She let him hold her there until saliva dribbled out of her mouth, her eyes teared up, and she had to grip his leg to come up for air. And when she gasped for breath upon coming up, she felt the rumble of his chuckle beside her.

"You're such a good, *sweet*, girl…" he cooed, and she didn't understand how those words sent her pulse into overdrive.

As he made a slow turn onto the highway, he grasped her chin so that she was looking at him, and he wiped away the tear that had escaped when she hadn't been able to breathe.

"Make me come, baby," he whispered. "Make me forget I'm driving this car. Send us both into oblivion."

A fleeting kiss was pressed against her lips, and she went down again. He tugged on her hair as she worked him, causing a tingle to rise on her skin and her pussy to throb. Sucking on every inch and swirling her tongue. But this time, she wasn't teasing. She wasn't savoring. She meant to bring him to his end—*crashing* to that end. Crashing and writhing and begging her to stop as he spilled. She wanted his legs shaking and his knuckles white against the steering wheel. Wanted him gripping her hair until she cried out.

"Shit, baby—"

She could feel the car speeding up as he tried to deny his end. And it only made her more eager. She had him right there, and could feel him straining and his hips bucking slightly into her.

"Oh, fuck, like that," he was suddenly saying. "Holy gods, Chloe—Like that—*fuck*—"

The engine was at a roar. They were swerving, speeding,

and every second had her taking him further into her abyss. His head threw back into the headrest as an urgency took her over. His hand slammed into the steering wheel as he cursed her name again, his cock taut. She had him—*had* him—

He spilled with a loud groan, and his hand slapped her ass so hard that she felt it quake in her bones. But she didn't stop. He was trembling, moaning her name like it was his saving grace. The car was slowing as she devoured his cum, swallowing and continuing to suck until she had taken every last drop.

"Shit—*Chloe*—"

The car stopped. Both his hands pulled her up by her hair, and she couldn't stop her devious laughter from sounding as she sat back on her knees in the passenger seat.

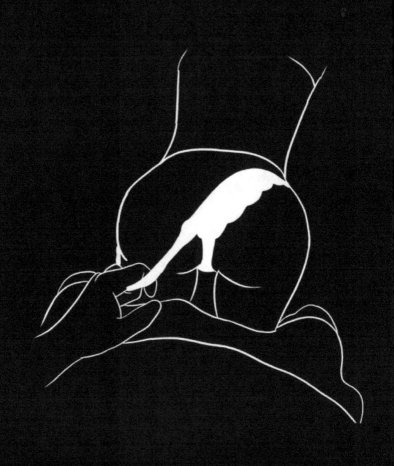

Holy fuck.

He'd had to pull over.

He hadn't come that hard in years, and she'd swallowed it like it was nourishment.

They were on the side of the highway, hazards blinking.

And she was grinning at him like she'd just won the fucking lottery.

A dribble of his cum seeped from the corner of her beautiful mouth. Her stained scarlet lips were smeared. There was a gentle spray of her mascara beneath her glistening, yet delighted, eyes.

He fought to catch his breath and clear the stars in his eyes as he put the Jeep in park, and he nearly ripped the seat belt out of its lock to get to her. She was magnetic... *poison*... a drug he would consume like water the rest of the night. Her mouth had felt like ecstasy. The memory of everything she'd done with her tongue had him twitching again. He leaned over and kissed her hard, groaning when she pushed her hands into his hair and her short nails scratched his skin, making him wild.

He was out of his seat in a second. Over her. Pushing her back. Grabbing her hips and pulling her legs in the air. He needed to feel how wet she was from that because he had a feeling she was drenched.

He loved being right.

Fuck, she was *soaking* through those panties. Her nails scratched his neck as he continued to kiss her. He could have ended her so quickly, he realized. He knew she was close just from what they'd done. He kissed her lower, sucking on her skin and tasting the sweat in the dip of her collarbone. He wanted to lick every part of her. And he would. Fuck, he couldn't wait to have her completely—

"Gavin…" She arched her back into him with the moan of his name, tugging at the roots of his hair, and when he looked up, intent on kissing her, he had to pause.

There was a candy heart on her outstretched tongue.

TASTE ME

He groaned against her skin and glanced at the GPS.

Five miles.

A quiet huff left him, his lips quirking upwards, and he kissed her again. "I will, baby," he promised before sitting back in his seat.

"Put on your seatbelt," he rasped, and she narrowed her eyes. "Seatbelt," he repeated. "Five miles of road lie between me having you. If you think I'm driving slowly the rest of the way, you're wrong. Put on your seatbelt."

She didn't argue, and as the belt locked in place, he couldn't help from smirking over at her and whispering, "That's my girl," as he put the car in drive and jolted out onto the highway. The jolt of the car threw her back into the seat again, that fucking laugh coming from her mouth, and he reached over to her thigh as they sped off.

The noise of the engine humming at its limit mixed with the roar of his blaring music fueled his desperation for her. It may have only been a few miles, but it felt like a lifetime. Mainly when she spread her legs and moved his hand higher.

"Don't stop," she said in a begging moan that chilled his

skin.

Blood rushed to his cock again as he dipped his finger beneath the fabric. Her head arched back into the seat, and she grabbed her knees.

"Guide me, baby," he told her, pulling her hand between her legs atop his. "Show me what you like." Her wetness surrounded his finger as she moved it. Stroking down her, dipping into her entrance, then back up to her hardened clit.

"You like it right there?" he asked, and her hips moved against his hand. "You're so wet for me, baby. Tell me which building is yours," he said as he made a turn.

"Make a right—fuck, *there*," she breathed, and he wasn't sure if she meant his hand or the building. "Go around this corner—Building 3818—"

He squeezed her clit between his fingers, and her hand gripped onto his wrist. A low rumble came from his chest.

"You're so greedy, baby," he said as he swerved into a parking place.

He couldn't get upstairs fast enough.

She was out of the car before him, shuffling her skirt down and throwing her bag on her shoulder. Everything was a haze as he followed her to the elevator. He barely saw the other cars or noticed the apartments. There was only her. Only this.

The elevator dinged, and he grabbed her by the waist, unable to resist himself from kissing her with his palms on her face, her hands on his waist. They backed into the cage, and she broke free from him just long enough to press the button to her floor. He was on her throat, tasting where some of her drink had spilled onto her skin, his fingers once more lifting that damn skirt up.

"How many floors do we have?" he asked her.

"Ten," she breathed as she hiked her leg around his waist.

The doors closed, and he pulled back to smirk down at her. "Don't come, sweet girl."

"What—Fuck, *Gavin*—"

Her chin craned upwards with his name the moment he pressed two fingers inside her. Gods, she was wet. He had to remind himself not to take her all at once. He bit her throat, his finger pulsing in and out, thumb on her clit. Her moan sent him cursing. She bucked into his hand, and he could feel her walls throbbing.

"You like this, don't you? You like being watched?" he said upon hearing her whimper as she started denying herself. "Do you think the security guard is enjoying the show?"

He had noticed the camera over the door as soon as they entered. Chloe pushed on his neck.

"Shit—what—" But her body limped when he curled his fingers deeper inside her again. "Gavin—"

"Tell me you want me to stop," he said on her neck. "Tell me you don't want to be watched. Tell me you're not throbbing at the thrill of knowing someone is probably getting off to the sound of your beautiful fucking moans, and the sight of your open mouth." He pulled back, meeting her eyes, and she sucked her lip behind her teeth as she tried to suppress a moan.

"Don't stop," she said in a breathless high-pitch.

He chuckled softly, slowing his caress. "Go ahead, baby," he said. "Scream for me—" he pinched her clit in his fingers, making her jaw shake with her sagging mouth. "—Give your audience what they want," he whispered.

The elevator dinged, and Chloe flinched, nearly jumping out of his arms, but Gavin just laughed against her skin. He pulled his hand from beneath her skirt, feeling her whimper in his absence, and he brought them to his mouth to taste.

"Mmm…" he teased her, smirking crookedly. "Like candy."

Chloe with her lips on his, grabbed him by the sweater and pushed him backwards. They were out of the elevator, slamming into the opposite wall. A picture fell. A vase on the table broke. The wall vibrated. She was clawing and tugging his neck and hair. Lips smashing together with such recklessness that he had to remind himself not to bend her over the small table and fuck her in the hall.

Before he could, she moved from beneath him, breaking their kiss, and she took his hand.

One turn. Two turns. The red-walled halls reminded him of the neon at the bar, only adding to his desire for this woman leading him to her home. She was heading toward the door at the end of the dead, darkened hall, and she dropped his hand to search for her keys.

He hovered over her, forearm lying against the doorframe, the other squeezing at her hip. He couldn't wait to have her undressed and restrained on the bed. Couldn't wait to feel her skin flush to his, hear her moan without holding back... the fantasies filled his vision, distracting him from her fumbling figure, so much so that when she got the door unlocked, he had to snap himself out of his daze.

The smell of spiced vanilla air freshener hit him as the door opened. He almost fell when she turned and grabbed him by the shirt, yanking him inside. The door slammed, and she pushed him into the back of it, her lips meeting his.

Whatever papers she'd had pinned to the fridge fell to the ground. Her hair tangled in his fingers as he pulled her closer. Hand sliding down her sides, he grasped her ass and hauled her up onto his waist. Her breasts pushed into his face, and he buried his head between them, biting the top of her breast where he could see stretch marks on her skin, and the sight of them made him grasp her ass tighter. He groaned at the thought of licking every mark on her body, tasting every inch of her delicate flesh and savoring the taste of that swollen cunt. Fuck, he was already pressing against his zipper at the thought.

He lifted his head, intent on kissing her again, but she

pushed her hands to his face and held him steady.

"I need five minutes," she managed, her heavy breaths jagged between them.

He swallowed, chest heaving, and he nodded as he set her on the ground again. *A break.* That could be good. He could collect himself. Take a look at the bedroom and get his bearings.

"Five," he agreed.

But before she could walk away from him, he hauled her back into his arms, fingers pulling in her hair, exposing her neck. "If you even think about touching yourself in there, I'll punish you the rest of the night," he warned. "And not the kind of punishment you think you'll enjoy." He relaxed his grip and slid his hand against her cheek, thumb brushing her lip, and she opened her mouth to suck his finger. He felt a restriction in the back of his throat at the sight, remembering how she'd sucked on that cherry, how her lips had felt around his cock.

"Five minutes," she repeated. "Get the candy out of my bag."

The right corner of his mouth flinched. He leaned down, acting like he would kiss her again, but he paused as their lips brushed. "Three."

Chloe nearly fell to the ground trying to get her boots off once she was in the bathroom.

Fuck, the cold floor felt good on her flat feet. She sank her back against the door, closing her eyes and taking a minute. She could still taste his cum on her tongue, feel his lips like a brand on her neck.

She let the room spin as she came down from the adrenaline that had been the entire hazy evening.

Thank fuck she'd been drinking water between those cocktails. Even the bar felt so far away. Like it had been hours since they'd left. The memory of his hand between her legs filled her mind, his slaps on her ass as she'd taken him deep. She couldn't wait to do that again. She could taste his name already, and she slipped her fingers between her thighs just to see if she was as wet as she thought she was.

But even as she started to touch herself, a thought hit her.

He was wandering around her apartment. Alone.

Shit, when was the last time she cleaned the fucking wine stains off the carpet?

Being a workaholic, she rarely had guests over, and sometimes things simply got out of hand. Thankfully, she'd at least taken time to tidy up and clean the clothes off the floor a couple of days before.

Okay, breathe, she reminded herself.

She pushed off the door and started shoving the dirty towels into the bin, straightening up the sink. She took a swig of Listerine and let it swish in her mouth as she moved things around. And after she spat, she stared at herself in the mirror.

Dammit, she was a mess. Her lip stain was smeared, some of her mascara had stained beneath her eyes. Her hair was flat.

Three minutes.

She was well past that.

Music thudded the walls. It appeared he'd found her speakers and connected his phone to it. She nearly laughed as she imagined whatever it was he was doing out there on his own.

Good thing the neighbors are away, she thought.

A spray of dry shampoo to her hair. Cleaning off her smeared lips. Heat beat on her cheeks as the warmth of the apartment finally hit her, and she stripped herself of her sweater and skirt, leaving only the red and black lingerie on her body.

She loved this set. The thigh-high stockings and attached strappy belt that stretched over her abdomen to just above her belly-button. Sheer black thong and red and black push-up corset bra.

One last flip of her hair, and she gave herself a final look in the mirror.

Gavin wasn't on the bed when she opened the door. She squinted into the darkness, noticing he'd placed some of the candy hearts on the bed and turned on one of her bedside lamps. The music blared—music that had her feeling more aroused than she had been before.

Perhaps he was Cupid, she thought.

She found him in the kitchen reading over the ingredients on a drink from her fridge, and for a minute, she paused to admire him.

He'd taken his sweater off, showcasing the tattoos on his arms that looked like geometric suns, moons, roses, bow and arrows, wings... like figure drawings from Roman times, dissected and in segments. Soft tufts of ginger hair lightly sprayed his toned chest. She could even see a splattering of freckles on his shoulders.

Those fucking shoulders.

His hips were pushed forward, and she couldn't stop herself from biting her bottom lip as she leaned on the doorframe and took in the rest of him.

Gavin looked twice in her direction, apparently having seen her move in the corner of his eyes. The stare he held her with caused her thighs to squeeze. His tongue darted out over his lips, and he sat the drink on the counter.

"That was longer than three minutes," he said, and her lips twisted smugly in response.

"What are you going to do about it?" she dared.

Gavin shifted, his head tilting as he looked her wholly over, eyes lingering on her breasts, then on her hips, and she watched as a pleased look rose over his features that she wanted to slap off his stupidly beautiful face.

"Come here," he said with a gesture of his fingers, and the way he said it struck her in the pit of her stomach.

She prowled to him slowly, cursing her fluttering heart. When she reached him, he slid one hand around her waist, his large hand grabbing at her ass, the other tickling up her side... from her waist, to her ribs, to her breast that he cupped in his hand before continuing up to her neck. He paused for a moment, and tilted her chin back as she grabbed onto his belt.

That damn dimple appeared with a lift of his lips.

"Exactly how fucking tall were those heels?"

Her mouth dropped, and she shoved him as he laughed in her face. "You're such an ass," she teased. "I'm not short." But he grabbed her fast, his strong arms lifting beneath her backside. She was wrapped around his waist again before she had a chance to get away from him, and his lips were on hers.

Her ass hit the counter. He leaned over, hands pressed on either side of her—their kisses long and deep, unlike before when they had been a whirlwind of teeth and tongues. Just as she thought he might let that hand trail between her legs, he pulled back, and he dangled a small red satchel in front of her.

"Pick three," he told her, his voice a vibration on her skin.

A surge of excitement pulsed through her body and settled as warmth between her legs, a knot of it weaving in her chest. She reached inside the bag for the naughty candy heart, and then she sat them one at a time on the counter.

LICK ME

Fuck yes, she thought.

TEASE ME

Even he groaned at that one.

TASTE ME

Chloe frowned at the last candy. "That's the same as the first," she argued, tossing it back in the bag. "I'm trying again."

"Knew you were a cheater," he said as he squeezed her thighs.

And her heart dropped at the one she pulled out next.

BEG FOR IT

A devious chuckle left Gavin's lips... throaty and dangerous... and her heart constricted when she looked up at him. All green had evacuated his pupils, replaced with an abyss of pure lust that made her breath catch.

"Maybe I'll put that one back—"

He grabbed her wrist as she made to change the heart out, and even though she knew they were teasing, the look in his eyes caused her to shift. He reached behind him and pulled something from his pocket—

The handcuffs.

The red fur was soft against her skin when he latched it on her wrist, and she swallowed, feeling her eyes start to flutter as the anticipation swelled.

"Repeat after me, baby," he said softly. "Arrow."

Chloe frowned, but repeated the word anyway. "Arrow... what's that?"

"Your safe word," he explained, meeting her eyes. "Use it any time you're uncomfortable, and I will stop. No questions asked."

Chloe's heart stumbled, but she could see the seriousness in his eyes, and she made herself give him a nod. "Okay."

Gavin leaned in to place a kiss on her lips as he pulled her other hand and locked it in the other cuff, then stood back and started rubbing her thighs up and down again...

"So, *Chloe*..." That stupid smirk lifted his lips, and he popped the last candy heart into his mouth before he asked in a ravenous whisper,

"Are you ready to play?"

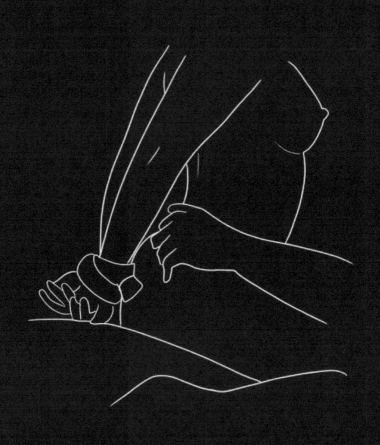

"Yes."

He stifled a groan at the word, at the whispered way she said it, and he leaned in to kiss her hard before hauling her into his arms and throwing her over his shoulder. A high-pitched squeal escaped her, along with his name, and he smacked her ass with such force that she flinched, and he swore he heard a soft moan come from her mouth.

He tickled his hand across her reddening cheek, squeezing that soft flesh, and then he spanked her again upon crossing into the bedroom. He threw her on the bed with a bounce, noting that smile on her face beneath her silky black hair. Standing back, he took in the sight of her in that lingerie again.

That *fucking* lingerie.

Gods, he'd almost forgotten himself right then. Had nearly thrown all intentions of teasing her out of the window. The way the black straps on her stomach and hips creased in her skin. How her cleavage heaved behind that bra as though her breasts wanted to be free. The stockings—fuck, the *stockings*. They wrapped her thighs like beacons telling him where to taste her first.

She rolled her head, her hair sprawling around her, and he sat on the edge of the bed. She looked at him, clearly confused, and he patted his thigh without uttering a word.

Chloe looked like she might argue as she sat up on her knees. "What—are you actually going to spank me?"

"Come here," was all he said.

Her brows knitted, but she shuffled his way hesitantly until she was knelt beside him, and when she paused, her eyes darting all over him, he noticed a delight in her gaze. He wondered if she knew she shouldn't be enjoying this, and she was anyway.

What a fucking treat.

"Did I do something wrong?" she asked innocently.

He grabbed her by the throat and yanked the handcuffs, pulling her forward so that she was just a breath from his face. She gasped, and he loosened his grip on her neck to wrap up around her jaw instead, feeling his smile lift at the sight of her pupils seeming to blow with both surprise and desire.

"You thought I was joking earlier…"

Chloe swallowed, tongue darting out over those red lips. "Yes," came her breathy response.

He resisted sucking her tongue between his own lips or biting that gorgeous pout. "Did you think you could be such a bad girl and get away with it?" he asked.

Her breaths were getting heavier, that delight waning just slightly from her eyes and turning into a deep lust, an almost *fearful* lust, but she didn't respond. Gavin chuckled sadistically, his fingers tightening on her face.

"Answer me, baby," he said, his sarcastic tone coming out in a gravelly voice.

"Yes," she said, a little faster than he expected.

His grip relaxed on her cheeks. "Gods, you're even fucking cute when you're scared," he whispered. Eyes traveling over her, he noticed the squeeze of her thighs, the tremble of her arms, the almost purse of her dry lips, and he wondered how much more wet she was just from that. He released her face, stroked her skin, and gave her a fleeting kiss that she leaned forward for again as though she wanted more when he released her.

"Over my knees like a good girl."

Chloe held his gaze as she stretched her arms in front of her, rising on her knees, and then she sank her outstretched arms to the mattress over his lap. Her ass wiggled in the air, making him stifle his own stiffening cock at the sight of her bent over him and waiting.

Shit, he wanted to take a picture of how fucking perfect this was.

Gavin trailed his fingers through her hair, his other hand grazing teasingly across her ass. His wrist flicked with his first slap, and Chloe jumped.

"Did you enjoy teasing me all night?"

Another.

But Chloe… Chloe didn't seem to care.

"Yes," she choked out.

Another, and he swore he heard a moan escape her, but he didn't comment.

"Did you take your time in that bathroom just to test me?" Another. *Harder*.

"*Fuck*—" an undeniable moan sounded this time; however, she tried to cover it up. "No," he heard her say quickly.

Her ass was reddening so fucking beautifully that he nearly forgot he should take it slow.

"Did you touch yourself in there?" He spanked her again, making her flinch.

"I—no," she answered, and he decided maybe that was enough for right then as he ran his finger between her tingling cheeks.

"Let's see how swollen that pretty cunt is…" He cursed as he felt her moan when he dipped inside her, touching her clit and swirling it slowly. "You're fucking drenching," he cursed. "Gods, are you always this wet?"

"Gavin—"

He tugged her up slowly, his hand still delicately touching her tingling ass, and he moved her legs to where she was straddled over his lap, pushing her handcuffed arms around his neck. Some of her mascara had smattered beneath her eyes again, and he reached up to smudge it with his thumb.

"That was only a taste," he whispered. "The next time you're over my knees, it won't be for pleasure. Tell me you understand."

Chloe's throat moved with her swallow. "Yes," she managed.

Gavin leaned forward and kissed her softly before muttering, "Good girl," against her lips.

Her eyes fluttered like they'd done at the bar when he'd held that candy on his tongue. She grabbed the back of his head and pulled him to her again, her needing lips crashing against his. He shifted her flush against him and let her consume the moment.

A smile tugged on his lips when he felt her wetness again. "You're going to come so hard for me, baby," he whispered as he teased her nerves. She bit her lip, rocking against his hand, and she nodded vigorously.

"Yes," she gasped.

"I bet your beg sounds as delightful as that smart mouth."

Her shoulders fell as though she were just remembering their game, and her hands scratched in his hair, tongue licking her lips as she seemed to collect herself. She began to nod slowly, her breaths quickening, and she whispered a quick, "Yes," before kissing him hard.

He lifted her around his waist as he stood, and she held onto him, continuing to kiss him and let him do whatever he wanted. Those handcuffs brushed the back of his neck, and he knelt onto the bed with her. Her back hit the mattress, and he moved from beneath her jointed wrists.

She never took her eyes off him as his hands pressed into the bed by her breasts, and he hovered so close to her face that she leaned up to kiss him again, but he moved before she could.

"Grab those bars, baby," he said with a nod to her black railed headboard. "Don't let go."

Her fingers latched around one of the black bars, giving her leverage as she arched her back, and he chuckled at her eagerness. "You're fucking *greedy* for me," he teased as he pulled the key to the handcuffs from his front pocket. He unhooked one so he could link it behind the bar, and when she was secure, he took a moment to smile down at her.

"You look so sexy like this," he said as he settled back on his knees between her bent thighs, his hands traveling up her legs. "Splayed out in front of me. Needy and waiting…"

"Gavin…"

"Arch up," he said, and she did, using the rails as leverage and lifting her back off the bed. He unhooked the clasps of her bra, groaning at the sight of her freed breasts, and he pushed the bra up until it hung over her head behind a pillow. She gripped those rails again, her body lifting in his direction as he held her gaze and lowered his mouth onto her taut nipple. Her lip sucked behind her teeth, her head throwing back, but he reached up and took her chin between his fingers.

"Eyes on me, sweet girl."

She needed him to move faster.

She was sure she would climax the moment he moved her underwear. Shit, she had nearly climaxed bent over his lap. Each slap had sent a pulse through her core and down into her already throbbing clit.

His mouth was back on her nipple, making her body rock as he sucked and squeezed the tautness between his teeth. One arm beneath her, while his other hand traveled down her side, pausing to grip her hip, her ass, the thigh of her bent leg. Her arms were already starting to ache above her head at the slow pace he was going. Every time his tongue swirled on her nipple or he teased her, she bucked her hips against his, utterly desperate for that friction between her thighs.

He chuckled against her skin, tongue flicking her breast, as the very tips of his fingers slid over her inner thigh.

"Is this what you want?" he asked. His breath heated over her wet peak, those fingers practically dancing between her folds.

"Yes," she cried.

"Yes, what?" he asked in a stern voice.

Her open mouth snapped shut at the demand, her next inhale jagged, and she met his commanding eyes.

"Please…"

The corner of his lip lifted again, and he whispered, "That's right, baby," before returning his full attention back to torturing her. Just his middle finger stilled over her clothed, yet throbbing clit, and she felt a needy breath leave her.

"Gavin…"

"Gods, that's beautiful," he whispered, sucking on her breast again. "Keep saying my name, baby… Every time your greedy little pussy wants more, say my name. Beg for it."

She was going to scream his name if he tortured her any longer.

"Please, Gavin," she found herself saying as she lifted her hips toward his hand.

He held her gaze when he finally moved her underwear to the side. His open mouth stilled over her breast, only his tongue flicking over her nipple, and she groaned as she watched that tongue move, felt his finger brush her clit. Imagining that tongue on her and doing the same to her sex.

She strained against the handcuffs, desperate to move her arms and push him between her thighs or thread her fingers in his soft hair. Something more than this.

"Taste me," she whispered, chin stretching. "Cupid… Eros…"

He groaned on her skin, his eyes fluttering a moment, and then he pushed up and kissed her. As though those names had made him weak or triggered something inside him. He pulled at her thong, and just as she started to pull away and tell him to undo the stocking clips, he dug a finger into the lace, and it ripped.

She gasped into his mouth, making him smile against her lips, but before she could say something about him ripping her underwear, he plunged a finger inside her, causing all thought of the ordeal to go amiss.

"Fuck, baby," he muttered as he pulled back to hover over her, his eyes landing on his hand between her legs. He met her gaze again, and she felt her mouth sag as he inserted a second finger inside her. Her eyes rolled with every slow thrust, every press of his thumb on her clit. She lifted her hips eagerly, saying his name again as she felt her walls tightening.

"Don't come yet," he told her.

She whimpered in response. Her arms were trembling. "Gavin…"

He thrust his fingers hard inside her, making her wince. "Not yet," he said again as his digits curled in her, tantalizingly hitting that spot and making her eyes roll. *Shit.* She was melting in his grasp, willing to plead and cry, and she lifted her hips.

"Gods, you're eager for that end," he rasped. "Say my name again."

His words only made her bite her lip harder. She called out his name once more, her back arching into him, and he was smiling wickedly at her when she opened her eyes.

"Do you want me to taste you?" he asked.

She bit her bottom lip and nodded vigorously. "Yes," she said just as he opened his mouth. "Yes, *please*, Gavin."

He huffed, glancing down at his the way the light caught off his soaked digits when he pulled out of her, and then his lashes lifted to her again as he tasted her on his middle finger.

"You beg so well, sweet girl." His pointer finger danced over her lip, her juices glistening on his skin, and his brow arched down at her. "Open your mouth," he said softly. "Lick yourself off my finger. Taste that sweetness."

She did, and she hummed around that digit, holding his eyes and watching his pupils widen, his tongue darting out over his lips. She ached for his absent touch, and he smiled down at her as if she had just completed his favorite task.

"My perfect girl," he whispered.

Fuck, she was going to come just from his fucking words.

He kissed the tip of her nose and shifted from over her. She couldn't breathe as he sat up to his knees between her bent legs. His hands stretched on the backs of her thighs, making her hike them into the air, completely exposing her bareness down below, and Gavin groaned as he stared down at her.

"Look at you…" he breathed, his thumb trailing dangerously close to her sex. "That pretty little cunt glistening…" His head tilted, lashes lifting, as he grazed that digit over her throbbing clit as he held her gaze. She flinched, and that smirk lifted higher.

"You look like my favorite candy, baby."

The words caught her off guard, breaking her briefly out of her daze, and she felt her brows knitting together. "What is your favorite candy?" she asked.

His only reply came in the form of his dropping to his stomach and hoisting her legs over his shoulders. "Do you know what I like to do with my candy?" he asked, his nose nudging against her folds, his heated breath teasing her sensitivity… It took everything in her not to tighten her thighs around his head and urge him closer. Stop this teasing and give her the orgasm she so desperately wanted.

"What?" she managed with a silent gulp.

He held her gaze as he placed soft kisses on her inner thighs. "I like to savor it… one lick at a time…" He was toying around her, making her breath falter every time he looked like he would take her in his mouth. "…until every bit of the hard shell is gone, and that warm center melts in my mouth…"

The throaty way he spoke was the most addicting sound she'd ever heard.

The right corner of his lips elevated as he kissed her entrance, and then he met her eyes. "Will you melt for me, baby?"

Her jaw was practically shaking as she whispered, "Yes."

That damn smirk met her, and she watched as his nose brushed against her folds, followed by more soft kisses on her inner thighs... And the first time his tongue stroked her clit, she limped into the mattress.

Deliberately, he licked her. Tasted her. Feasted on her. Every stroke of his tongue and suck of his lips sent her spiraling. His fingers dug into her ass as he held her there... Fuck, she wanted to pull his hair and have him suck on her until she made her lip bleed from holding back her release. He made her feel like *she* was his favorite candy, and her head threw back when his tongue circled inside her.

She squirmed and cursed his name every time she was forced to suck in a jagged breath. His tongue felt like it was made for her. Her body began to roll against his mouth, legs beginning to shake as she felt that climax cresting.

"Gavin..." She grabbed that rail behind her head, her arms totally numb. A whimper left her as she tried to deny herself from coming all over his face. She didn't want it to end. She wanted him to taste her the rest of the night.

"Look at me," he whispered against her skin, kissing her thigh. "Watch me while I feast."

She did, and she nearly fell apart at the sight of him pulling her clit in his mouth and sucking, holding her eyes with his. She didn't know how she could possibly get wetter, but she knew she had. He reached up around her body and grasped her breast, squeezing as he gripped her thigh tighter in his other hand. Tongue torturing her in the best way. Her heels dug into his back, toes pointing as she pulled on the handcuffs. She needed to grab something—*anything* to help her keep her composure. Another whimper choked from her, and she began to tremble.

Tears glistened her eyes. Her entire body tightened to the point she thought she might break—

He slipped a finger inside her. She bucked against his

hand, feeling that finger slipping so effortlessly in and out of her as he continued his tongue tease. She cried out, her arms straining…

"Gavin," she pleaded. "I'm going to—"

"Not yet, baby," he told her. He moved his finger from her pussy and stretched that digit between her cheeks, searching for her other entrance, and then he tickled his finger over it.

"You wanted me to tease you," he whispered, a soft chuckle leaving him. "Let me tease you." He kissed her clit, and as he did, he slipped his fingers inside both entrances, and a chill rolled over her skin.

"Oh, god, *please*," she cried out.

He chuckled against her entrance, plunging deeper inside her, and she dared to meet his delightedly dark eyes. "That's right, baby," he practically growled, tongue darting out over her clit. "Say my true name. Call on your lustful god to bring you to your end."

She didn't care if he was Cupid or Gavin or Santa or the fucking tooth fairy.

She was going to scream for him. She would scream for her release.

She jerked against the railing headboard so hard that she heard the bed creak. She was lost—out of body.

"Gavin—"

"Beg for it, Chloe," he demanded as he picked up his pace, his fingers hooking inside her. "Beg your god."

She did.

She pleaded with words she didn't know she was saying. Her body quaked down to her core. Every tease from the moments before came crashing down on her. She picked her hips up off the bed, eagerly moving with his tantalizing strokes. Until he sat up on his knees and started thrusting his fingers in and out with such vigor that her entire mind blanked. Picking her up off the bed, he placed his other hand around her throat. He was hovering over her, his thumb on her clit, broad chest flat against the back of her thigh.

Pleasure ricocheted through her, and a tear fell down her cheek. She was reaching, reaching—*reaching*. She'd never felt her body in such a strain. His fingers on her throat tightened beneath her jaw, making her vision cloud. A numbing sensation trickled over her skin with a violent tremor.

And when his breath hit her cheek, she couldn't hold herself together any longer.

"Let that pretty pussy rain, sweet girl."

Her climax hit her like a slap to the face. She released with a scream. His hand was off her throat and from inside her, and before she could even finish coming, his mouth was back between her legs, and he was feasting on her like his last meal.

Tongue lashing inside her and draining her juices. Sucking her clit, making her convulse even harder. Her legs were a flinching mess, but she could do nothing about his continuing to torture her. It was pain and desire unlike she'd ever known, a worship even, and she kept coming again, before she could stop herself. Until she saw spots in her blurring vision, and she nearly began to cry from the overwhelming sensations.

As he finally straightened over her, she tried to catch her breath, snifing back her exhaustion and swallowing her tears. Golden light hit the back of his figure, and for a brief second, she thought perhaps she *was* looking at a god.

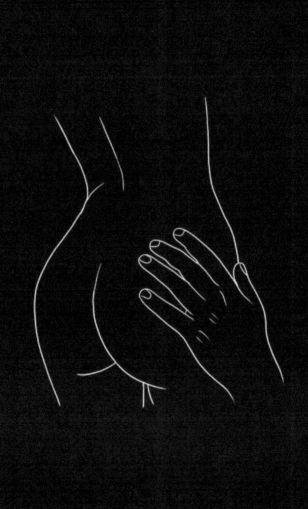

13 GAVIN RIDE ME BEND ME OVER MAKE ME CUM I WANT YOU

Gods, she was beautiful.

Her moan was a sound he wished he could put on repeat. The look in her eyes as she denied herself, the taste of her cum on his tongue, how her body responded to him so well...

He released her wrists from the handcuffs, knowing her limbs were exhausted from straining, and she limped against the mattress, soft groans leaving her as she continued to come down.

A quiet smile parted his lips when he picked up his sweater from the floor with intention of putting it on her.

"Can you hold your arms up for me?" he asked.

"Fuck you," she muttered, and a laugh Gavin hadn't felt in a long time left him.

"Right—" He lifted her arms one by one, eventually able to get the sweater on her and pull her hair out from the back. As he started to pick her up into his arms, though, she reached for his face and pulled him down to her lips.

He had to take a moment, surprised by the action, and he caved into her desperate kiss, dropping her legs back onto the bed and holding her cheek while his other entwined in her hair. It nearly sent him onto the bed with her again. Fuck, the things she did with her tongue had him needing her more. His cock was already throbbing from watching her come, and

79

this kiss… wasn't helping matters.

But he knew she needed to take a break, and he forced himself to wrap his arm under her knees and pick her up off the bed. He took her out into the living room and placed her on the couch. And when he finally pulled away from her, he turned on the TV.

Some reality show that he hated admitting he knew a lot about came up on the screen. He snickered under his breath as he made his way to her refrigerator. He'd been reading ingredients on the drinks in the fridge earlier when she'd come out of the bedroom, grateful that she had turmeric coconut water to stay hydrated.

For a few seconds, he merely pressed his hands into the edge of the counter, regaining his breath and trying to force his hardened cock down. He didn't know how long she would be out, but he knew if she touched him within the next few minutes, he was going to come before he could stop himself.

Snap out of it, Gav, he told himself. *She's just another mortal. Think of terrible things… like your mother—*

Gods, if she saw him like this, she would have a field day.

"Shit," Chloe was muttering as she sat up. "What just happened—"

Gavin smiled, pulled himself out of his daze, and poured Chloe a large amount of coconut water into a cup. She was stretching her fingers as though trying to get the feeling to return to them when he reached her. He stilled at the sight of her sitting up in his sweater, mascara smudges beneath her eyes, her hair out of place and frizzed in the back from where she'd been laying.

He swallowed at the sight of her there, in all her raw glory, remembering every noise she'd just made, every look of her scrunched up face, and her biting her lips. His stomach began to twist at how vulnerable and exposed she was right at that moment, and how beautiful it was seeing her in such a bare state.

He extended her the drink without saying a word, and then he sat on the coffee table in front of her. Her fingers were shaking upon taking it, and he bit back amusement as she gulped the liquid down, holding the cup with two hands. A dribble of water made its way down her chin, one that she didn't bother to wipe off when she relaxed back in the seat, her cup sitting lightly between her legs. He reached for her foot, pulled her calf into his lap, and began massaging it while she seemed to collect herself.

She closed her eyes for a few minutes, flinching every so often with his kneading fingers, and he thought she might fall asleep right there. Until she finally rolled her head, cracked her neck, and she opened those heavy eyes to look at him.

He had to run his tongue over his dry lips as he held that spent gaze. "Okay?" he finally managed to say.

"Great," she said as she took another sip of her coconut water. "I think I'm still coming. What did you do to me?"

He chuckled under his breath and pulled her other leg into his lap. "Baby, I'm just getting started," he promised.

A small smile rose on those pouting lips as she sat up, taking her leg away from him. He reached forward to wipe the mascara that had streaked beneath her eyes, and she looked like she might laugh.

"I'm a mess, aren't I?" she asked, amusement in her tone.

"You're fucking gorgeous," he said without hesitating, his voice hardly louder than a whisper.

As their eyes locked, that knot tightened in his stomach. Her doe eyes dilated, a faint blush on her cheeks, and for a split second, he wondered why the statement seemed to still her.

"What?" he asked.

"Nothing," she said. She looked down to her drink, her

hair falling over her face, and with a bite of her lip, she leaned toward the table and grabbed the bag of candy hearts.

"I believe it's your turn," she said, dangling it in front of his face. "Choose them while I learn how to walk again."

He chuckled at her as she rose to her feet, her balance wavering slightly—enough that she reached out and grabbed his shoulder—and then she made her way to the kitchen. He couldn't help himself from watching her bend over into the fridge and grab something from the inside.

A string cheese stick.

She grabbed a couple of them, munching on one, and made her way back to the couch as he shifted onto the cushions and pulled a heart from the bag.

MAKE ME CUM

She made an 'ooo' noise, her mouth full, and she sat sideways on her knees at his side. He laid the candy heart on his knee and pulled out another.

BEND ME OVER

"That one is for me," she teased, her arm linking around his neck, nails scratching softly on his neck. He resisted the urge to grab her by the waist and pull her on his lap right there. But he decided to wait for that as he pulled a final heart from the bag, and he groaned at the words.

RIDE ME

"Fuck yes," he heard Chloe mutter. Her hand landed on his inner thigh, her lips brushing his jaw. She slowly stroked his leg before reaching around for his hand, and she placed it on her thigh. His eyes fluttered at the pressure of her hand through his pants, and with every movement, he squeezed her flesh tighter.

"You don't want a break?" he asked, still feeling her thighs shake.

"I've wanted you inside me since the elevator," she admitted, making the hair on the back of his neck stand.

"And I always get what I want." She shifted, her breath tickling his ear as she whispered, "Even from gods."

Gavin nearly lost it.

She began to place featherlight kisses down his throat. He reached for her neck, tugging slightly on her hair, and she groaned against him as he pulled her head directly in front of him. He watched as her eyes rolled, a quiet 'ah' coming from her parted lips when he gripped her hair. She leaned forward, her teeth grazing his lip, and then she pushed up to her knees, throwing her leg across his waist. He kissed her hard, his mouth moving down her throat as an urgency took over. She was already grinding on his thighs, her body rocking against his, holding his head in the crook of her neck. He pulled the shirt over her head, capturing her breast in his mouth and causing her to groan out his name.

Her lips met his as she fumbled with his belt. He took over, giving her ass a hard smack as he said, "Sit up on your knees for me," against her mouth. She did, and he sucked on her nipple, letting her stay distracted as he shuffled his pants off beneath her. His stiff cock bobbed upon its freedom, and as she sat back on his knees, she grasped him with both hands.

"Fuck, baby," he muttered, both his hands slapping her ass hard again and making her wince. He did it again and again, each time causing a sharp gasp to emit from her throat, and he chuckled into her neck.

"My sweet girl likes her ass red, doesn't she?" he said, fisting her ass.

Her grip tightened around his cock in response, making him curse her name, and her own smile spread as she whispered, "Don't stop," and she rocked her hips against him. She had her breasts pushed up between her arms as she delicately moved her hands up and down his length.

Every time she stroked him, he had to hold himself back from taking her. She squeezed his tip, precum spilling over, and his hands tightened even more on her flesh in response. Her bottom lip sagged as her eyes fluttered from the sensation. He leaned forward, tugging her bottom lip between his teeth, and she turned the motion into a biting kiss that made him pull her flush to his chest.

She consumed him. He was lost in this, in *her*. Her wetness grazed his throbbing cock, his groan drowning into her mouth at the sensation, and she pushed off his lap. He watched as she sank to her knees, those fucking eyes staring dangerously up at him as she raked her hands up and down his bare thighs.

"I didn't get to watch you in the car," she said in a tantalizing tone.

He caught a mouth-watering glimpse of her ass, and he cursed at the irresistible way her skin was prickled red from his slaps. Fuck, the sight had his own skin tingling. *He* had made her ass red. *He* had marked her flesh and claimed her. And she… she had responded *so fucking beautifully*.

He couldn't wait to mark her more.

He tore his eyes away from that masterpiece and back to her face. She pushed her hand in her hair and pulled it over her right shoulder, exposing her neck as she leaned up. And when her tongue touched his cock, he swallowed and closed his eyes.

"Eyes on me… *Cupid*."

He huffed a laugh that turned into a cursing groan when her lips wrapped around him. She tongued his slit, making that knot in his stomach tighten. "That's right, baby," he gritted out as he fisted the edge of the cushions.

His hips pushed toward her as she went deeper. That familiar heat surrounded his length, and he wasn't sure how long he would be able to last being able to observe her this time.

"Take me deeper, baby," he whispered as he wrapped his

hands behind her head. He pushed her scalp, watching his cock disappear entirely into her mouth and feeling her choke. "*Shit*—that's it—"

He released the tension on her hair then, and grabbed the couch instead, letting her set her own pace, and occasionally forcing her to take him deeper. Every time he watched her bob down, his cock slick with her puckered lips, he felt himself falling. She pushed her breasts around his length, bouncing a few times on him. He groaned, feeling his cock almost straining at how insatiable he was for her at that moment and soaking in the way she looked up at him.

"You're a dirty girl, aren't you?" He grasped the back of her head again. "You want me to fuck that mouth?"

The hum that vibrated him in response went straight to his straining dick.

"Yeah, you do," he chuckled. "Open wide. Let your god have you."

His hips lifted, and he fisted her hair and held her steady as he watched his cock move deep in and out of her mouth. Watched her salivate around him and felt her gag with every thrust. She drew her lips tight, trying to keep up with his movements, and he strained at the sight of her hollowing cheeks and the feeling of her nails scratching his thighs.

She was so fucking magical; it took everything in him to stop. He made himself sit up and pull her mouth off and capture her lips with his own, knowing he was done for if she continued. He reached between her thighs and moaned into her mouth when he felt her wetness.

"Gods, you're drenching again," he whispered. "Is this just from sucking my cock? Do you want it that badly?"

"Yes—" she wrapped her fingers around his length, her thumb swirling on the slit. "I want you inside me."

Those words surged him. He took her lip between his teeth again, biting and holding her eyes until he saw her wince. His hand wrapped around the back of her head, and he whispered, "Ride me," when he let her go.

Her lips crashed into his again, and as she stood, he wrapped his hands to her ass and gave her another hard spank that made her groan into his mouth. Her mouth was furious against his, tongues clashing, holding his hair and tugging like she wanted him closer. She sank over his thighs, one leg at a time, before pushing her clit against the tip of his length.

He leaned forward to suck her nipple into his mouth before muttering, "Please tell me you're on birth control," and he settled his chin on her breasts as he looked at her with pleading eyes.

A soft laugh escaped her as her fingers pushed his hair back off his forehead. "I wouldn't have invited you back here if I wasn't," she told him, and relief swept through his body. He kissed her chest in response, and she rocked against the tip of his cock. "Are you ready to come for me?" she asked.

Gavin sucked in a sharp breath, calming himself at her tease, and he tipped her chin back with his knuckle. "No, baby," he said as he positioned himself at her entrance. "You're going to use me."

Chloe eyed him, her hips rocking tantalizingly against his cock. "Am I?" she said in a breath.

"I can get off at the mere sight of you. I want you pleasured." He shifted slowly beneath her, spreading her cheeks and holding her ass at a hover as he slowly started sliding his hips up and down, the tip of his cock tickling just inside her drenching entrance.

"Use me, sweet girl," he breathed out. "Take your pleasure. Let that greedy little pussy feed."

She kissed him recklessly, and his entire body caved when she sank onto him. Her tightness stretched to allow him in, and he found himself cursing as she slowly worked up a rhythm.

She was so tight around him. Wet and consuming. Shit, she was perfect around him. The way her breasts pushed and fit against his chest. How her flesh melted in his hands. He squeezed her hips, muttering out her name and aching at denying himself from coming too early. Gods, she felt amazing, and every time he heard her sharp gasp, he held her tighter.

Her shoulders tensed up, mouth opening, jaw quivering... "Fuck, right *there*," she whimpered out, her hands tightening at the back of his neck, her breasts pushing against his collarbones as she took what she needed.

"That's it," he said, holding at the bend of her hips and watching that pleasure spread over her beautiful face. "That's my girl," he breathed, "Give that cunt what she wants."

It took everything in him not to throw her onto the couch and haul her legs in the air, finish fucking her in a manner that would have had her pleading for her god again. But he held her hips instead. He sucked her breast. He cursed on her skin and squeezed her ass, and he let her find that spot inside her. He let her use him for everything she wanted. Because watching her face and seeing her take it had him rock hard and begging, and he loved seeing her like that.

She threw her hands around his face and kissed him hard, her rocking becoming faster and faster. He could feel her walls tightening, noticing her breaths turning to gasps, and as she reached that edge and started to cry out into his mouth—

He pushed her back, grabbed her around the throat with one hand, and slapped her ass so hard with the other that she startled aloud. Her entire body jerked, her mouth open wide as she tried to cry out, and he held her there—she came all over his cock as he thrust hard in and out of her and squeezed her throat. His cock glistened with her release with every stroke. Fuck, that was beautiful. His eyes lifted back to her face, watching her eyes roll, her mouth open like she was gasping for breath. He slapped her ass harder, and with her nails digging into his chest, he, too, came crashing down.

He spilled inside her and released her neck. That knot in his stomach wove up his chest to his aching heart. He grasped her forearms and pulled her torso against his, and as she limped into his grasp, she kissed him with stolen breaths.

But even as they both fell from their releases and shook against one another, she didn't move off him. He held her against his chest a few moments as they settled, as his cock finished twitching inside her, and when she pulled back to look at him, he couldn't stop himself from kissing her softly.

This woman…

"I should… I should go clean up," she whispered when she met his gaze again.

Gavin nodded, his chest still heaving against hers. She slipped off him, and for a moment, he stared at their combined juices on his cock and spilled over the stretch marks on her inner thigh. A low groan escaped him at the sight of it.

So fucking beautiful.

Every movement in the bathroom made Chloe ache, and she couldn't stop smiling about it. Fuck, she hadn't been satisfied like that in... well... *ever*.

And they weren't even finished.

But she was done with this particular lingerie. The stocking clips were starting to dig into her flesh, and she was sure there would be marks in her skin from the strappy belt.

It was snowing again when she looked out the window from her bedroom. Having grown up where she didn't get to see snow often, she couldn't help admiring it for a few moments. She could practically feel the chill of it on her skin despite the warmth of her rustic apartment.

Her phone lit up in her bag by the table where Gavin had left it, illuminating the inside of the purse and brick wall behind it, and Chloe realized this was probably the longest she'd ever gone without looking at her phone. She shuffled out of the belt and the stockings before grabbing it off the nightstand to see who had messaged her.

Having fun?

Lana.
Chloe shook her head at the screen and replied back.

Did you make it home safe?

Just got here. Wanted to make
sure the serial killer hadn't
driven away with you into the night.

Chloe laughed.

I'm not dead yet.
No promises. You might find
my body in the morning,
though.

I'll check in before work.
See you tomorrow, Clo.
Have fun ;-)
I hope he's doing everything to
you from those filthy books.

Well, he's not a demon,
but I can't be picky

LMAO
Clo!

He swears he's a god
Eros, to be exact
Cupid

Is he?

I haven't decided.
Maybe

Damn girl
You found a god?
I need to hear this

Save me details

> I'll see you tomorrow. Ice
> cream time.

Lol the essential
between fucks snack

> Obviously
> Who did you take home?

Total loss :-(
That's okay
I can take care of myself

> What about that last
> one? David?

Too drunk to function

> Ouch

Exactly
See you tomorrow, Clo
Enjoy your god ;-)

> Night, Lan

Chloe closed out the phone and went to her dresser, intent on finding something a little more comfortable, yet still sexy, and she finally decided on a pair of lace, high-waisted cheeky panties and matching balconette bralette. It was the only bralette she'd ever been able to find that genuinely fit her breasts, and she loved it. She put on fuzzy socks as she grabbed a bottle of water from her nightstand, and then she made her way back to see what Gavin was doing.

He was still on the couch, though he'd put his skinny dark jeans on again and was drinking the rest of that coconut water while watching whatever reality TV had popped on the television.

His music was still playing on the speakers, softer, but she could see him moving his head to the music as he watched the show. He was so sexy sitting there on her black couch, the brick wall behind him seeming to highlight his dark ginger hair. The only lights coming in were from the neon signs across the street, the lights from the other buildings there and down below, and from the TV. He must have shut off the kitchen light when he grabbed a drink from the fridge.

She smirked at the sight of him seeming so at ease there, and as she cracked the lid on her water, she leaned sideways against the door frame.

"Cats or dogs," she asked, and Gavin finally noticed her.

His gaze darted wholly over her a moment, and it was clear he hadn't been paying attention to what she said.

"What?"

"Cats or dogs," she repeated.

Gavin had to adjust himself as she stalked toward him. Shit, this outfit was even hotter. Then again, at this point, he was sure she could make trash look sexy.

"Ah... dogs," he replied upon her reaching him.

She reached onto the couch and grabbed his sweater, and when she leaned over, she paused in front of his face, smiling widely before kissing him in a lingering manner that were he not trying to recover, he would have pulled her onto the couch again.

She pushed his sweater over her head then straightened to go back into the kitchen. He grabbed her ass as she left, making her jerk; a quiet laugh escaped her lips, but she kept going. Gavin leaned back and watched her walk, allowing his gaze to travel over her pear-shaped ass, watching it jiggle as she opened up the fridge.

"The car that you would give your right testicle for?" she called out to him as she bent to peer into the freezer.

"No, not the right one," he said as he grabbed his chest. "That's my favorite."

She lifted a brow at him over the freezer door, and he scoffed.

"Black sixty-seven Chevelle," he answered.

Her lips puckered, making an "ooo" sound as she emerged from the freezer with a pint of ice cream. "Had to be the sixty-seven though."

"Would be the sixty-nine—"

"If it wasn't for that damn nose," she finished, grinning widely at him.

He chuckled under his breath, surprised that she knew the car at all, and he was even more curious about the ice cream in her hand. Although, as he continued to watch her, he couldn't help playing along with her questions.

"Job at sixteen," he asked.

"Veterinary tech," she answered. "Ruined my entire desire for the field." She grabbed a spoon from the drawer. "Ice cream?" she asked, holding up a spoon.

Gavin mockingly rubbed his abs. "Surprised you have to ask after that round."

Her smirk widened. "I hope you're not completely exhausted. We still have quite a few hearts to get through," she said. "What was it you said at the bar... that you planned on doing each of these to me? One by one?"

He ran a hand through his hair, feeling as though the bar had been a lifetime ago. "My plans haven't changed," he promised.

She closed the drawer with her hip and left the lid to the ice cream on the counter before making her way over to him.

"I have a bad habit of eating ice cream on nights that I'm up late," she said as she crawled onto the couch at his side. "Mostly leading up to the holidays. Big sales and all. Everyone needs a graphic for every little thing..." She licked a heaping mound of the ice cream off the spoon. "It's the fucking worst," she said with a full mouth.

He chuckled at her, and she dug another heaping teaspoon out, holding it for him to eat. "Ice cream and reality tv," he said as he leaned forward and licked the cookies and cream flavor. "Shit habit of mine as well."

"God, doesn't it make you feel better about yourself?" And the brutal honesty of her tongue made him laugh. She sighed back against the cushion. "This is the first night since last summer that I haven't been buried behind my computer," she admitted. Her head rolled and she looked him over. "You're a terrible distraction."

His smile widened. "Distraction is something I'm good at."

She shook her head at him, taking another bite of ice cream, and she turned her attention to the TV. He grabbed the other spoon and ate some of the delicious treat himself.

"What is it that you do?" he asked.

"I'm a graphic designer," she told him. "Freelance work. I have a lot of clients around the states. I do all my work from home. I get to travel occasionally, so that's fun—oh wait, I love when she does this—"

He chuckled as she mimicked a scene from the show, having seen the woman on TV make a particular gesture before, and then Chloe slumped back against him.

"What about you? What does the *god of desire* do in his free time?" Her eyes locked with his in a comical way. "Or does he have a day job?"

"He has a day job," he replied. "I'm an app developer."

"Oh? Anything I've heard of?"

Besides the most popular dating app out? No.

But he resisted telling her.

"Maybe," he shrugged.

She snickered. "So, you're mysterious now?" she teased. "You're not ready to divulge all your secrets to me?"

"Give me another round," he joked. "Then we'll talk."

"You know what we should do," she said, and he squinted at the look on her face.

"What's that?"

"First, we should order pizza," she said. "There's a place

downstairs that delivers up at all hours of the night. And second, we should leave a bowl on my balcony out to catch some of this snow. It's coming down pretty hard. We'd have enough for snow cream in an hour."

"What is snow cream?"

Her eyes widened as though he'd just uttered the worst thing he could possibly have said. "What—you don't know— oh, this is a *tragedy*."

She was on her feet in a second, the ice cream forgotten about, and she retrieved a silver bowl from beneath her cabinet. He started to ask what she was going on about as she reached him again, but she just grabbed his hand and pulled him out onto the fire escape landing.

Snow fell around her as though her gravity were pulling it to her. She placed that silver bowl on the step, and then stepped up to the banister.

Gavin beamed at her there. Her head thrown back, his sweater hiked above the lace underwear as she held her arms wide, that look on her face, her tongue stuck out as the snow landed on her...

He took his phone out and snapped a photo of it.

"What's the name of your pizza place?" he asked her.

She moved to his side, huddling against him for warmth, and he let her type it in. She had the order ready for payment within a few minutes, and he just laughed when she offered to pay.

"Never happening," he said, snatching the phone away. He entered in the last three digits of his card for security, and as he put it back in his pocket, he told her it said it would be up in thirty minutes.

She gazed at him with a coy smirk that made him want to kiss her again.

"Thirty minutes... Whatever will we do to occupy the time?" she teased.

He trapped her between his long arms, making her lean back on the iron banister, her leg bending as she smiled up at him.

That *fucking* smile.

Gods, where had she come from? How was he so in need of her?

But he tried to keep himself together.

"I suppose we'll just sit around and watch more of your reality TV," he shrugged.

"You say that as though you wouldn't enjoy it," and the way she laughed made his stomach knot.

"I have another suggestion," he said, voice dropping.

"What's that?"

He leaned forward, tickling his nose against her cheek, watching as her mouth opened, and she let her hands settle on his bare chest. Her eyes darted from his lips to his eyes, and just as he leaned forward almost like he might kiss her, he said in a breathy tone,

"Tell me about this snow cream."

She snorted, clapping her hand over her mouth as she chuckled at the turn in conversation. "And here I thought you were being broody," she jested.

"I can be broody," he said. "But you have me very interested in why we're collecting filthy snow in a bowl."

"It's something my family always did," she said. "We used to sit the bowls on our cars when the snows came because we only ever got snow every few years. But you can't collect it from the ground. You have to let it get in the bowl like this. I learned that the hard way. You take the snow and mix it with sugar and condensed milk. It has to be the right amount though. Otherwise it turns to mush, and ice cream makers help out a lot, but... we would just mix it in a bowl."

There was a glisten in her eyes that he didn't understand, and he wondered why the mention of it had made her sad when she'd been so excited only moments before.

"My dad used to bring home a can of that milk any time the forecast even mentioned snow... No matter how late he had to stay out on call, even in the middle of a storm... He always brought it home for us." She sighed heavily and looked up, letting the soft flakes hit her cheeks for a long moment, and Gavin reached a hand beneath her shirt to squeeze her waist.

"Shit," she muttered, blinking fast. "Anyway," she continued, seeming to compose herself. A smile flashed on her lips, her hands slapping softly on his chest, and her lashes lifted. "It's a good thing I grabbed a can at the store yesterday," she added, and he knew she was deflecting from whatever it was that had just bothered her.

"Now, I get to show you what you've been missing out on all your life."

"I think I've been missing out on a lot," he said with a sigh, deciding not to push the subject. "I mean, polluted snow sounds extremely appetizing—"

She smacked his chest, and he laughed out loud, swinging back slightly as he held onto the railing, continuing to mock her. "—Especially the snow that you clearly scooped off the ground. We should try that now—"

Her mouth agape, she picked up some of the collected snow from the rail and threw it at his face, and as she bent out of his grasp, he pulled her back in, and his lips crashed down on hers.

It was smiling and laughter that lingered between them and that kiss. Swaying with each other beneath the falling flakes, and holding on in a moment that seemed to lull. He could taste the cold on her skin, the water on her chilled throat when he moved his lips. The laughter faded, leaving behind kisses and soft sucks of breath from her in his ear that made his shoulders limp. Her nails scratched the back of his head as she held him in her neck, her back leaning over that railing.

He grabbed her bottom and lifted her to sit on the banister. Her thighs tightened, a squeal leaving her, and she hugged her arms around his neck.

"Gavin!"

"I got you, baby," he promised.

A few snowflakes melted on her face as his hand landed on her cheek. He took another few seconds to look at her as a soft wind blew through her damp hair and brushed his skin. But with a smile, she leaned forward to kiss him again. Slower this time, the chill around them barely apparent with the heat rushing through their veins. He slid his hands under the sweater to grasp her tighter, deepening their kisses and spiraling as his need for her grew. Their lust heightened with every kiss, to the point that he couldn't get her close enough to him. He needed her. No games.

This woman…

And when he finally pushed his finger between her thighs to her warmth, he decided that was how he would survive this chill.

"Hold the rail and raise your ass," he said as he pulled back.

"What—"

He kissed her hard and moved her hands himself, pressing them onto the cold banister. When he stilled in front of her, he watched as she sucked that pouting lip behind her teeth again, holding his gaze as he moved his hands to the top of her underwear.

"Squeeze your thighs around me and lift, sweet girl," he told her.

She did, and he pulled her underwear down over her bent knees, but stopped upon noticing how she was squeezing her toes around the rail to hang on. He chuckled under his breath and grabbed her knee. "Unhook this," he told her, playfully shaking her leg.

"Gavin, I'm going to fall—"

"I have you," he promised as he stroked her calf. "I'm not letting you go."

And there was something about that statement that wove the knot back in his stomach.

She seemed to consider the words as he held onto her other leg, and finally, with her arms straining, she unhooked her toes. His smile widened, holding her gaze, and he leaned forward to kiss her pink nose as he pulled her underwear off her foot.

"That's my girl," he rasped. "Other leg, baby."

He stuffed her underwear in his back pocket as he kissed her again, squeezing her legs and rubbing them up and down until he trailed one hand between her thighs again. He felt her heated wet center, causing a groan to escape his lips.

"Gavin…"

His lips were on her neck, more eager for her upon feeling her, and he knew he needed to taste her again. He wanted to bury his face in that heat and feel her hands in his hair as she dangled on the edge of disaster. He wanted to feel her pulse and legs jump every time she wavered off balance. He could feel her trembling, and whether it was from the chill or the danger, he wasn't sure.

He lowered to his knees, holding onto her legs the entire time, and he jerked his head up at her when she grabbed his hair and pulled. There was a questioning in her eyes, and he knew a thrilling fear had entered her.

"Squeeze your legs around me—" her calves tightened behind his arms, which he still had on the outside of her thighs, "—just like that… Hold the railing or my hair. You're doing so good, baby."

Her eyes fluttered as he leaned forward and kissed each of

her thighs.

"Don't let me fall," she whispered.

He smiled, his hands tightening around the tops of her thighs. The vulnerability in her eyes, the snow coming down around her and landing in her hair, the street lamps and red neon lights behind her... He found himself retracting his previous statement that he'd seen her at her most beautiful state.

"I have you. You're all mine."

He held her eyes as he shifted forward, and with his first kiss on her clit, her shoulders limped, and her hands relaxed just slightly in his hair.

Every stoke of his tongue made her moan, and he memorized her twitches, her sounds, and her taste. She was his favorite flavor yet. And after a few moments, he wondered if she forgot she was sitting on two inches of railing... outside with the neighbors just a few feet away.

She cried out his name once, and he chuckled against her, sucking her clit into his mouth and making her gasp, and her thighs shake.

"That's right, baby," he said between tortures. "Tell your neighbors who you belong to."

She cursed the air, her voice a little softer this time, but she didn't tell him to stop. Her fingers tightened in his hair, her breaths becoming shorter and shorter. She was trying to move her hips, but one hand shot to the railing as she eventually remembered where she was.

Her jaw dropped, and he watched her face scrunch in that beautiful way that he liked—that he *knew*... He teased her with his tongue, in and out, savoring that wetness and heat against his face. He could tell she was getting close by the way she was moving... *shaking*...

"Fuck—Gavin—I'm going to—"

She didn't even get the words out before her hands

clenched in his hair and her thighs tightened so much around his face that he couldn't breathe. Though, he didn't care. She was spilling on his tongue, and he drank her like he was starving.

His knees were soaked and numb. She was still quaking when he held her legs and pushed back up to his feet. A familiar daze in her eyes met his when he straightened in front of her, as though she were under a trance, then she threw her arms around his neck and kissed him hard.

Desperate and needing. An ache pulsed from his heart down to his twitching cock. He slipped his arms around her waist, finding her skin soaking with the precipitation coming through his sweater.

He curled a hand around her freezing cheek and pushed her damp hair back when they parted. "Shower," he said in a breathless rasp, nearly choking on the word, and Chloe's short black nails grazed his cheeks as she huffed out a laugh, her air visible between them.

"Hot shower would be amazing."

Getting back into the apartment was a stumble.

There were chills on her flesh from the freezing snow, heightened by the things he'd just done. Her heart continued to pound, her toes numb.

But she couldn't stop kissing him.

She wrapped her legs around his waist, and he carried her inside, his feet tripping over the plant on the floor. He caught his balance before they could go tumbling down and pressed a hand to her cheek as her wet feet touched the ground. The warmth hit her skin from the heat of her living room, and she felt as though she were melting into his arms. His kisses were long, yet needy. She needed to feel his bare skin against hers. Wanted that hot shower raining over them as he took her against the wall or bent her over.

Barely parting from one another, she reached for the hem of her shirt. His breaths whispered against her wet skin, warming her up with every kiss down her throat. She tripped on the coffee table when he kissed her hard again, but he caught her by the waist and for a moment, they swayed, soft chuckles coming from their throats. She was on her toes, needing to have him engulfed around her, as he grabbed her ass and squeezed. Every clutch of his hands on her flesh had her chilled body vibrating back to life.

She couldn't tell if she loved or hated the erratic pace of her aching heart and the way it seemed to burn in her ears and her chest, how her muscles felt restless from his every touch, and she couldn't seem to get him close enough.

Damn him for making her feel this way.

But, fuck... *Fuck*, it felt good to be wanted.

She reached for the button on his drenched pants, not daring to break their kiss, and together, they pulled them down, his stiffening cock bobbing free and hitting her abdomen before he bent over to try and finish taking off his jeans, fumbling on the bottoms. Her bralette was flung off. She grabbed his face and kissed him again, steadying him, and when he kicked the heavy jeans to the side, he finally grabbed her fully around the waist and lifted her onto his waist again.

Bare skin flush, they slowed as if the contact alone had electrified their connected souls. She could feel his hard cock grazing her entrance as he moved with her. She didn't know how he knew where he was going, but he side-stepped the coffee table, his hands massaging her ass, making her buck against him with every squeeze.

The doorbell rang.

It was as though that fucking chime drenched their minds back to reality. Gavin cursed under his breath as he pulled away from her lips, and she slid down his body to her feet. He rested his forehead against hers, swallowing as he regained his breath.

"Turn on that water for us, baby," he whispered. "Get ready for me."

Chloe had to remember to breathe when she went inside the bathroom. She turned on both the overhead shower and the removable shower head. Reality swept briefly over her as she felt the cold water on her hand.

Her heart throbbed in her ears as she willed her breaths to

even, closing her eyes and holding to the glass door handle a moment to try and collect herself. Steam began to billow from the water, and Chloe reached out to touch it just as she heard the door snap close.

Gavin had paused, his hand still on the door, and she straightened as she remembered why he had parted from her to begin with.

"Did the pizza guy enjoy this view?" she teased, her eyes traveling over his body and landing on his stiffening cock. She had to squeeze her thighs at the sight of him again, staring at the trail of his ginger curls below his abs, the heave of his stomach, and the appearance of those straining veins beneath his forearm tattoos.

And it was such a nice cock, too.

A devious smirk flinched his lips, and he began to slowly stroke his dick. "Asked if he could join," he said in a low tone.

"I hope you gave him an extra tip and told him he could stay to listen for my screams outside the door if he wanted," she bantered.

Gavin scoffed and started towards her. "Baby, you're going to scream loud enough he'll hear you in his shop downstairs."

"Sounds a little far-fetched," she couldn't stop herself from saying.

"It's a promise."

His arms wrapped around her, and he dipped low, his kiss evacuating the breath that had just tried to enter her lungs, and he started walking her backwards into the black-tiled shower. The heated water rained over their heads, making goosebumps rise on her skin.

He was over her, aggressive hands worshiping her like it was their job. Teasing her taut, sensitive nipples and grabbing her flesh as he kissed her neck to her collar, lapping up water on her skin down her chest.

She surrendered, losing all fight and nearly going limp as she allowed him to take her. To flip her and press her chest into the steamed wall, his hand moving around her hip to her wetness. She could feel his hardened length rubbing between her thighs. His other hand slid up to the back of her head, his large fingers massaging and gripping at the roots of her hair just tight enough to make her mouth sag, her head to sink into him as he held her, and as his chest pressed hard against her back, she felt him smile against her neck.

"Give me this," he whispered upon his finger dipping inside her. "Tell me you're mine."

That digit swirled over her aching clit, his hand tightening in her hair, and she lifted her foot onto the bench. One hand reaching behind his neck, the other between her legs. For a moment, she guided his hand over her clit, and then she reached for his length that was grazing her entrance. He cursed into her neck, his teeth dragging over her flesh, and she stroked him.

"Yours," she managed, turning her head slightly. "Take me, Eros. Show me *my god*."

Every muscle in his body seemed to tense around her. She still wasn't sure she believed him, but as he kissed her jaw, she felt as his grip moved to her hip, and he squeezed.

The hand in her hair tightened and pulled her back to the point that he had her throat fully exposed, making her suck in sharply, goosebumps rise on her flesh, and he whispered in a voice that sounded desperately like a growl,

"Put me inside you."

He released her with a jolt. His tone shuddered her to her bones, and she did what he said. He pressed on her back to make her bend lower, and as she moved to slip his cock inside her, she felt his fingers bruise in her hips.

"Fuck, you're perfect," he muttered as he sank torturously

deep and stilled there. "Hold that wall, baby. And Chloe?"

"What?" she managed as her hands flattened on the tile.

"Make sure the people downstairs hear you."

She wondered if the people in the building across the street could hear her.

Every thrust had her fighting her weakening muscles. His cock buried deep, hitting her spot and filling her body. She pushed back on the wall, trying to hold herself steady there, but with the water pounding on her back and numbing her skin, she began to lose herself.

"Oh, you scream so well for me, baby," he whispered, and she felt his hand traveling up her spine. Reaching into her hair again, he yanked her up by her roots, and she relaxed back against his chest as he slowed down.

Every time he pushed inside her, she fell more under a trance. The heated water spattered over them, misting their bodies as their movements synched. His breath on her neck. His fingers entwined with hers on her stomach. His lips hit her neck, sucking and marking her beneath her hair, and when he pulled from within her and flipped her around, she had to grasp around his neck to keep herself from falling apart.

Her back slapped into the tile. He aggressively hitched her legs around his waist again and sank his cock deep. Shit, he felt like a dream. Filling her up totally and hitting the most delicious spots in her that had her aching for him to never stop.

His hands moved to her hips and he lifted one thigh higher than the other, encouraging her to shift with him. "Shit—*Gavin*—right there—" she managed to get out.

She felt her edge growing with every deliberate stroke, but she held herself back. Her nails dug into his skin, open mouth catching water as she sank her head back against the wall. His lips were pulling blood to the surface on the pillow of her breast, to the point she felt a high-pitch gasp leave her at the pinch he had on her. Her body tightened around him, and she heard him curse on her skin, whispering, "Not yet," in a pleading tone.

"*Gavin*—" Her muscles staggered again as he kissed her, sucking on her tongue and her bottom lip, making her moan into his mouth. But he wasn't wrong. She didn't want to come yet either. She never wanted to feel the cold air on her skin. Not if it meant she would be absent of this.

So, she held herself at the precipice longer. He rocked slower, holding the back of one of her thighs higher so he could push even deeper. His sack hit her ass with a purposeful grind of his hips, as if he knew exactly the spot he was hitting and how it was making her feel. She was shaking, her toes pointed—

"*Fuck*—gods, you feel so good, Chloe," he whispered on her flesh. "So fucking good—"

"Gavin, I need to—"

His kiss swallowed her words. He thrust inside her the deepest he could, and she gasped into his mouth. He cursed again, and she felt him suddenly picking up his pace and steadily rising. Gripping her ass, her neck.

"Please—"

"Let go, baby," he finally said.

Her jaw shaking, she heard a noise leave her that she didn't recognize. Her entire body tensed. Her nails broke his skin. She cried out once more and succumbed to that blissful state again. She crumbled around him, her orgasm spilling over with a vigorous shake. His strokes quickened even more, and she watched with an open mouth as he came inside her.

For a moment, they stilled, their now heated bodies rising and falling in unison with one another. The look on his face when he came was a sight she wanted to watch over and over. The way his brows scrunched and the deep curse of his moan. She reached out, pushing his hair back off his forehead as she watched and felt him finish twitching.

Gavin let go of her ass after a few more seconds, and after he slid out of her, he pressed his hands into the wall by her head, pinning her there as they continued to calm. His eyes closed, he rested his forehead to hers.

"Who are you," he said in a breath she almost didn't hear, and she wasn't entirely sure what he meant. However, she didn't press it, and instead simply kissed him.

Gavin continued his slow torture when he finally rubbed her down with soap, making sure to get into every little crevice and cranny of her body, taking eager care with more sensitive places. His lips pressed to every part of her as he doused her in her citrus soap. Bubbles held on her tender skin. He treated it like he was painting her, and she laughed when he drew a bow and arrow on her stomach.

"Okay, *Cupid*," she teased, grabbing the soap from him. "Let me."

She'd never had fun bathing with another person, but she did with him. Her hands roamed every part of him, taking special care with his cock, stroking him back to life and making him groan when she had him hard in her grasp again.

She reached for the removable shower head and took it down as she moved her hand over him slowly. The speed of the water moved to massage, and she let it beat down at the base of his neck and his shoulders as she pumped his thick cock.

Gavin cursed and started to reach for her, but she made him press his hands into the wall and glass door, threatening to get the handcuffs if he tried to touch her. That fucking smirk lifted his lips, but he didn't move as she brought him to his end. A broad, wicked smile—the same that had found her in the Jeep—held on her face at the triumph of his cum shooting over her belly and in her hand.

Fuck, he made the best noises. And the look in his eyes when that gaze skated over her after completion had her heart fluttering.

She dragged her finger through the cum on her stomach and locked eyes with him as she licked it off. Gavin looked like he might pounce on her: shoulders tensing, eyes hardening… She wondered how much restraint it was taking for him not to grab her immediately, but he seemed to be patient.

He slowly took the shower wand from her hand as he composed himself, whispering, "Come here," to her before dragging her against his chest.

It was a dangerous command—a challenge—much like when they'd first started their game, and Chloe's heart skipped at the way he looked at her. His lips landed on hers, distracting her as he moved that wand over her shoulders and back, down to her hips and the curvature of her ass…

And when she felt him move the shower spray between her legs, she flinched out of his grasp.

"Gavin—"

His brow raised, almost as if he knew how powerful that would be against her already sensitive clit. He lifted his chin, a crooked smile rising as he shifted the shower spray to a more gentle setting.

"Let me clean you up."

A laugh escaped her as he teased her with the spray, and before she could get away or open the shower door, he grabbed her by the waist and into his muscular arms again.

"Is this your favorite—Is this what you do when you can't go to sleep?" he mocked, and she grabbed onto his arm, smiling into his shoulder because that was all she could do. Her thighs were jelly, and she was wilting from the pleasure catching up to her.

He sprayed that heavy pressure against her clit again, making her jerk, and she began to fall apart.

"Do you get in this shower and hold this water on that swollen clit until you can't feel your legs? Do you imagine that shadow, baby? Do you imagine that faceless being while you sit on this bench and pleasure yourself?" he said on her skin.

She was shaking as he moved that pressure, hitting her in every place that had tears pricking her eyes. She wasn't sure how she was supposed to come again. Her vision blurred. She was collapsing. His grasp tightened around her waist, holding her steady. She was grateful for the grip, as she was sure without it, she would have been on the floor.

Every time that water moved over her throbbing clit, she jerked. Her arm wrapped under his, hugging his bicep, with her mouth on his shoulder. She cried out his name in a whimper, and he steadied that water on her clit. Letting it beat and torture her in the best ways. Somehow, this was what would be her end. This would send her tumbling in a way that completely numbed her mind and body.

"Let go, baby," he whispered on her skin. "Relax for me. I've got you. Give me this orgasm. Give me all of you."

She tried to. She *wanted* to. Her heart felt like it might stop. Every part of her body strained. Her knees were shaking. She was sure she was drawing blood from his skin. And when he kissed her in that irresistible way he'd kissed her out on the balcony, she finally gave in. She let go of denial. She stopped holding back. Wails left her that she wasn't aware that she possessed.

"That's it," and she could feel his muscles tightening around her, his hand clutching her hip like he was holding her up. The water pressure sent her body convulsing—

Chloe crashed. She screamed and couldn't stop herself. She cried out into his collar, her knees gave way, but Gavin caught her fast. He let the shower handle fall and verberate against the wall as she came crashing down, her body jerking and whimpering, tears springing down her cheeks. Her entire body radiated an ecstasy she'd never felt before. Euphoria swam throughout her every pore, and she wondered how anything else might match the bliss she felt right then.

"There's my sweet girl," he whispered as he kissed her nose. "You did so well, baby."

Chloe nearly collapsed in his arms after he towel-dried her hair. He carried her into the living room and laid her on the couch, a pillow under her head. He pulled one of the blankets out from the basket by her television and placed it on her as well. He didn't eat the pizza, but he did set it out on the table, along with a couple more coconut waters and regular waters from her fridge, before crawling onto the couch himself and tuning into the TV.

He couldn't sleep. Even with how tired he was, he continued to stare and wonder about her. How she had come into his life mere hours ago and it had felt like he'd known her a lifetime. The window remained open. He could see where so much snow had collected in her bowl that it was overflowing. A soft chuckle left him, but as he started to get up to bring it inside, she sat up and groaned an unintelligible mutter. She hardly looked at him before shifting to her other side, and she laid her head in his lap like he was her favorite pillow.

The blanket fell to the ground, so he tugged it up and wrapped it back over her. He couldn't help reaching beneath it, though, his fingers absentmindedly rubbing her exposed flesh at the top of her thigh, the bend of her hips. He'd put his sweater back on her and the high-waisted underwear, along with a new set of thick fuzzy socks that he'd seen hanging out of her dresser drawer.

She was a fucking goddess lying in his lap looking exposed like that. *Vulnerable*... And a knot twisted around his heart as he reached for his phone to check for messages.

Thirty new emails. Ten texts—most of which were from his friend Zayn asking for details. More notifications from various apps. And finally, his reports on Cupid's Arrow.

He thumbed through the texts and emails quickly before moving to the reports. Everything was up. The party had done a great job exposing more people to the app and helping people find their match. Gavin closed the reports and instead opened up the app to see what he could toy with. He'd hardly had any time other than playing with Lana's matches earlier in the night.

He'd just shifted a match together when he felt Chloe move in his lap.

"How is your lap this comfortable," she muttered in that breathy voice that sent his hair standing on end.

He squeezed her flesh and gave a playful slap on her hip. "Sleep, baby," he told her.

But she shifted up beside him and laid her cheek on his shoulder instead. "What are you looking at?— Are you—" She pulled away abruptly and stared at him, suddenly totally awake. "Really? You're looking at that app when I'm lying practically naked in your lap?"

A tease, but he did ponder if perhaps someone had ignored her like that in the past.

"Curses of being a workaholic," he said with a sigh.

"How is that app considered work?" she asked.

"It's my app," he replied.

She nearly balked. "What? What do you mean it's *your* app?"

"It's my app," he shrugged. "I developed it."

114

And this time she was staring at him like he'd grown another head. "You're *Gavin Erosin?*"

He chuckled lightly. "Does that matter?" he asked with a tilt of his head.

"You…" She shifted to sit on the edge of the seat, and he felt his eyes narrow at her.

"What?" he asked.

She blinked as though she were taking it in, and then she slumped her hands in her lap with a soft laugh. "Shit," she finally said. "I could make a lot of money with stories from tonight."

Gavin laughed at the jest in her tone and delight in her eyes. He never led with his name or even told some people that part about himself. He liked parading in secret rather than being at the front of the brand in headlines.

"I could see it on the front page of the tabloids while I sat on a yacht and sip my martini," she continued to tease. "*'Gavin Erosin seduces woman with promises that he is a god.'*" She laughed at him, and he shook his head. "Too bad I'll never see that headline."

"Why's that?"

"I like having you as my secret more."

And there was something about the statement and the look in her eyes that made him reach out for her hand and kiss her knuckles. His stomach twisted at how she was smiling at him. She huffed a soft chuckle, her hair falling over the side of her face.

"Pizza is getting cold," he told her.

"Oh, I forgot about the pizza." She turned and reached into the box appearing as if she were starving. When she slumped back into the couch and took a large bite, her eyes closed like it was the best food she'd ever experienced.

"Mmm… fuck, this is good—Sorry, did you not have any yet?" she asked as she looked over at him.

Gavin laughed quietly and waved her off before reaching for his own slice.

"This show is still going on?" she asked upon seeing what was playing.

"Must be a marathon," he said.

"I love this episode—" she laughed at the antics on the TV, her mouth full, and she reached for the remote to turn up the volume. "Have you seen this one?"

He shook his head. "I haven't."

"Oh shit—" She was laughing so hard that she moved off-balance, and he couldn't stop staring at her. But eventually, her laughter faded, and on her third slice of pizza, she slumped back into the seat again.

"This pizza is so good," she continued, eyes closing and satisfied noises coming from her. "*So* good."

"If I'd known all it took was pizza to make you orgasm, I'd have taken you to dinner first," he bantered. "Though, I'm not sure we would have made it through the appetizers. I wonder…" he continued as he tore off a piece of crust and popped it back, "how long do you think it would have taken the waitresses to notice my fingers sliding in and out of that beautiful wet pussy during dessert?"

"We lasted all the way to dessert?" she asked, brows elevating.

"I think I would have teased you just to see people watch," he said. "I would *love* to see people trying not to get off at the sight of that fucking face you make when you're about to come."

A confident smirk spread wide on her lips. "No, we would have taken dessert to go in your Jeep," she countered. "And I would have ridden backwards on that throbbing cock while you sped down the highway."

"Specific," he jested.

She chewed off another bite of pizza, smiling broadly.

"*Every* fantasy… or was that not what you promised me?"

He grinned at his own tease and reached forward for another piece of pizza.

The TV show went on, and together, they laughed. He almost choked on his food once, and she gave him a hard time about choking, to which he ended up pulling her into his lap and spanking her playfully after. And after a while, she situated her legs across his lap, and he took up massaging her calves as they sat up to watch shit infomercial TV.

"I don't want to work tomorrow," she said when things got quiet.

"Big projects?" he asked.

"Well… most of my clients are in fashion. Valentine's pretty much marks our launch into spring adverts. It's so weird to switch directly from sweaters and coats into shorts and tanks. But that's the industry here." She leaned on her hand, and he could see a fatigue taking over as she asked, "What about you? Is your office here or do you work remotely?"

"I do a lot of work remotely," he answered. "But, my home and office are in California." He paused to look her way. "I fly out in the morning."

A heavy sigh left her, and she sat up on her knees. "Can I literally tell you how relieved that makes me?" she asked as she shifted to straddle over his lap, their hands entwining together.

"That I don't live here?" he asked, his skin tingling at her fingers brushing with his.

"Yes," she replied. "I didn't want you to think this was going any further than tonight," she admitted. "I work seventy hours a week, mostly in my pajamas at home without showering for days in between," and he laughed at the admission, making her do the same.

A beat of quiet settled between them, and he watched her

face soften, a faint blush rise on her cheeks.

"I think you would be an awful distraction from what I want right now," she continued in a softer voice, "and I'm not ready to give that up or put myself in a position that would make it unfair to you."

"Not ready to, or unwilling?"

She paused for a moment, her hands toying with his. "Can I be totally honest with you?"

"I think I can handle that," he teased, and she smiled softly at him in response before sighing so heavily that her shoulders drooped, and she began to rub the insides of her wrist where she had a small raven tattoo on her pulse point.

"After my last relationship, I think I'm completely terrified that I'll lose myself for someone again," she admitted. "I lost everything about who I had become. It's like this switch just turned off, and I became someone I didn't know. I shut out my family. I stopped talking to friends. And after that relationship ended, I didn't know who to be. I had lost so much during that time that I had nowhere to go and no one to turn to. I fell into this... *hole*. I threw myself into work and everything I could get my hands on. I drank... I cried... I tried things that..." Her voice trailed, a glisten rising in her eyes, and she glanced up at the ceiling.

"And then one day, I looked up, and years had passed." Her voice was shaking, but she just shook her head as she stifled back whatever emotion had threatened to surface. "I have worked *so* hard at finding myself again," she said. "I finally got my family back. I found a job that I love that is on my own time... I found reading and nature again. A couple of friends who are actual friends and not just pretending... The thought of someone coming in and taking that from me is..." She stared at his shoulder, almost in a trance, exhaling audibly as she continued to brush her thumb over that tattoo.

"I just can't lose myself again," she finally said as she

finally met his gaze.

Gavin didn't say anything. He wasn't sure he was supposed to. So, he continued rubbing her thigh, and after a few seconds, she laughed softly at herself and wiped her cheek.

"You must think I am a complete basket case now," she said.

He chuckled under his breath, and he reached out to cup her face in his palm. "I think you're real," he whispered.

She covered his hand with her own, holding his eyes. "Tell me why I feel comfortable saying all of this," she asked softly. "Is it your stupid magic? Are you using glamour on me?"

A tease, he knew, but he hadn't used his powers all night. Everything had just been *them*.

But he would play along.

"You know what glamour is?" he asked.

"Of course I know what glamour is." She smiled. "I've read Percy Jackson."

He laughed aloud. "The minotaur erotica makes sense now," he bantered.

She blinked, apparently considering it, her smile widening. "You know I hadn't thought about that, but I guess it does." Her laugh filled the apartment, and he held onto her as she continued to shake her head at herself. "Oh, isn't it funny the things from your childhood that progress into fetishes and kinks?" Her head tilted, lip sucking behind her teeth, her eyes brightening up at him.

It was so fucking cute that he considered changing his flight the next day.

"I've always found that fascinating," she continued. "How your childhood can mold so much about your life."

Just as she opened her mouth to go on, she sat up suddenly, her wide eyes shooting to the balcony, and she bolted off the couch to the fire escape balcony, coming back inside with the heaping bowl of snow after.

"We have *so* much snow," she declared, making him smile at the look on her face. "Help me make it?"

Helping Chloe make a favorite childhood treat of hers was like stepping into a domestic bliss he'd never felt before. He leaned back on the counter while she worked, occasionally helping out with mixing or tasting, and he had to admit the flavor was enticing. Or maybe it was that the delight on her face was so enthralling that the shit snow could have tasted like his least favorite food, and he would have loved it anyway.

"We have to let it freeze," she told him as she bent over to close the freezer drawer, licking her fingers when she straightened.

"Least favorite game as a child," Gavin asked, continuing with the random questions.

"Oh, that's easy," Chloe said as she piled up the dirty spoons. "Duck, duck, goose."

He laughed. "What—why?"

"I was always scared of getting chosen and then having to get up to run or chase someone. I hated it."

"Such a *spoilsport*," he teased.

That smile broadened on her lips. "Accurate," she chuckled. "I used to get so embarrassed. It took me a long time to get over it," she admitted. "One day I just decided, fuck it. I don't care what others think of me. I still don't like public games like that, but... at least now if I trip over my own feet or say something awkward, I know how to own it." She turned to run her cold hands under the water and then leaned back on the counter.

"Favorite holiday—besides Valentine's Day," she added, smirking at him. "Surely the god of desire has another holiday he likes."

"Halloween," he answered.

"Oh? What do you do on Halloween? Dress up with a bow and arrows?"

He eyed her mocking face and shook his head. "Usually working," he answered. "Something about that holiday…" He shifted on his feet, his arms wrapped around his chest as he thought about why he liked it. "The entire vibe of it. Its history…"

"The unknown," she added, meeting his eyes. "Dangerous and full of mystery. Dark… It's perfect."

A soft silence padded the room as they watched one another, and Gavin switched the weight on his feet. "Ideal date," he asked.

She eyed him sideways. "What a surprise that Sir Eros himself wants to know a girl's ideal date," she mocked. "Shouldn't you know that by all the app data you've collected?"

Gavin scoffed and pulled his phone out to search for her profile. "Your profile is quite literally blank," he said as he turned the phone around. "With the exception of this one photo—"

She chuckled at the photo of her eating a cherry, one eye closed like she was laughing, wearing a white tee and her hair down, and she shook her head as she reached into the fridge for a drink.

"Do you like ciders?" she asked, pulling two from the inside.

"Are you dodging my question?" he asked upon taking the drink from her.

"I am, yes," she answered, popping off the lid and taking a

long swig.

His brows elevated as he watched her continue to try and avoid him, until she chuckled out loud and almost rolled her eyes.

"I honestly hate dates," she admitted. "They're so awkward—at least the first few. It's like each one is a new job interview."

"What would you prefer instead?" he asked, amused by the admission.

"This," she blurted, almost as though she couldn't stop herself. Her broad smile faltered like she hadn't meant to say it. He watched her uncross her ankles and press her foot into the bottom cabinet, holding that drink against her chest like she was trying to make herself smaller.

"I prefer this," she continued. "I prefer feeling a connection in person and chasing it."

"What if I took you out?" he asked. "Where would you want to go?"

And he knew it was a gamble to even mention it after what she'd admitted about not being ready. She was likely to push him out of the apartment right then, but he was willing to chance it.

She smiled at the floor and then up to him, obvious she was about to shut him down. "Gavin—"

"Hypothetically," he said fast. "The romance novel version."

She scoffed and pressed her hand onto the lip of the counter behind her as she seemingly thought it through. "Okay... Ah... Autumn festival or carnival at night," she answered. "With the lights everywhere."

"Weather?"

"Oh, you can control the weather now?" she bantered.

"I might know a guy." A lie, but it was fun to make her think.

"Damp grass and chilling fog weaving through the forest around the outside. Just cold enough that I can wear a sweater and skirt with my boots and hat, and you could wear a sweater and leather jacket—obviously you have to have the jacket because at some point I would need it—"

"Obviously," he added, his stomach twisting with the vision.

She smiled wide and took another swig of her drink. "We would eat shit fried foods and drink sours and ciders all night. We'd laugh, maybe meet my friends, maybe get lost in the Hall of Mirrors, and you'd spend a ridiculous amount of money on those games trying to impress me."

"What else?" he asked, voice dropping.

She sat her drink on the counter and started towards him. "You would bribe the Ferris wheel operator to pretend the ride was broken," she continued. "Or to go very slow…"

He felt his chin lift as she playfully tugged at the belt on his pants, those doe eyes looking up at him. He stared down his nose at her and drifted his fingers along the outskirts of her arms. Lower and lower, the feeling of goosebumps rising on her skin with every whisper of his touch. From her waist and down to her hips.

"*Excruciatingly* slow," he said softly, one finger then toying with the hem of her underwear.

"The other people on the ride would begin to complain," she said. "Perhaps even panic at being stuck."

"Absolute chaos," he said, trailing lower.

"But we wouldn't know," she whispered as her eyes darted to his lips. "Because your hand would be between my thighs…" Her eyes fluttered as he dipped his fingers beneath the hem on the curve of her ass. "I'd try to be quiet as you teased me, but… in the end, those people would get a show."

"You would sing my name to the stars," he said upon gripping her flesh tightly. "That ride wouldn't be the only place you would come for me, though."

"No?"

He shook his head as he started massaging her backside. "I'd take you in the shadows between the performer trailers —with my hand over your mouth because the sound of that fucking moan would make people come running. And after I'm done... when your back is raw and your legs shake... you'll walk around bare... with my cum dripping down your beautiful thighs." His nose tickled hers with his words, and she pressed her hands to his chest. Her fingers curled, nails scratching his chest just enough to send a chill down his spine.

"I have one condition," she said.

"Anything."

"We get cotton candy before we leave."

He chuckled, swaying with her slightly. "As long as I get to eat it off you when we get home."

Her soft laugh met his, and he swore a faint blush rose on her cheeks as she stared at his chest for a quiet moment. A tenseness rose between them. One that made him squeeze her tighter against him, his brows knitting just slightly as he saw her swallow.

"Do you know what I think?" she asked, lashes hitting her eyelids as she lifted her gaze to his.

He didn't respond immediately. The look in her eyes had him concerned for whatever it was she was about to say.

"What?" he finally asked.

"I think..." Her eyes moved away from his, and for a brief second, she stared outside at the snow. "I think I could see myself getting lost again just to have you," she admitted in a whisper. Her gaze landed on him again. "And that scares the shit out of me."

There was a genuine fear in her breathless voice, and he leaned forward to rest his forehead on hers.

"I'll find you," he whispered.

Her hands pushed up to his neck. "Promise?"

"When you're ready."

Her lips met his then, and for a moment, he was there at that carnival. He was standing beneath the night sky with her. He could hear the noise of laughter and screams from the amusement rides. Fog hit his cheeks, a wind circling them. The smells of fresh, damp dirt and pine entered his nose. The taste of the cider on her tongue only furthered the vision. It was as vivid as a memory, not a fantasy. So much so that when she pulled back and he found himself back in her apartment, the reality jolted him with a skip of his heart.

"What time is your flight tomorrow?" she asked.

Gavin inhaled a deep breath, blinking back to her. "Nine twenty-two," he answered.

"That's very specific," she jested.

"You asked."

She hugged him a little tighter, yet lifted her chin up to see his face. "You'll be gone before sunrise, then," she realized. "You'd better hope this snow cream firms up. You have to taste this before you go."

He chuckled and leaned down to kiss her nose. "I will, baby."

Every time she kissed him, he felt himself spiraling further for her and forgetting reality. He grabbed her up behind her thighs and placed her on the counter where he'd just been leaning. Her soft laugh filled his ears as she leaned back, and he started rubbing her thighs.

"What's waiting for you in California?" she asked.

"Top floor condo… the beach… work…"

"Sounds terrible," she mocked.

"The worst."

Chloe reached for his hands. "Do you think we could extend tonight a little longer?" she wondered. "You say you're a god. Is there anyone you can call up and ask to stop the sun from rising as quickly as it will?"

He scoffed, thinking of the god he would have to call to make that deal, and he shook his head. "Afraid not."

"I guess I'll settle for your shadow in the dark then," she teased. "What will you settle for?"

He leaned forward, chasing after her as she playfully dodged his kiss, and he ended up burying his face in her neck. She hugged his head there, her nails scratching his scalp.

"This, here." He leaned up and placed a gentle kiss on her lips. "Every thought will be of my good... *sweet*... girl," he teased as he pulled back.

She groaned and leaned forward, her teeth scraping his bottom lip. "Call me that again," she said in a breathy tone. "Tell me I'm your good girl."

He chuckled. "That's not how it works." He gave her ass a hard slap, and then he reached behind her for the handful of candies he'd left on the counter.

"One more round, baby," he told her.

"Tired, Sir Cupid?" she jested.

"Exhausted," he said, smiling at her. "But I *need* to feel you around me once more."

He captured her lips in a lingering kiss, her arms circling his neck, and he held her close to him as he picked up the candies and held his palm open.

"Pick three," he said before kissing her jaw.

She closed her eyes and stuck her hand into the hearts, and for a final time, she laid the candies on the counter.

GOOD GIRL

"How did that get in there?" he asked, picking it up before she could claim it. He tossed it back over his shoulder, grinning in her face as her mouth dropped.

"What—no, that one counts!" she protested.

Her playful argument made him chuckle. He circled his arms fully around her waist, giving her ass another spank, his smile burying in her neck, and he started sucking her throat as she giggled and chose another heart.

BITE ME

"Interesting," she said, and he pulled off her neck to see it, smiling widely at the heart before her lashes lifted up to his.

"Last one, Eros."

The rasping way she said his name made a shiver rise on his skin, that knot in his stomach tightening to the point of almost pain. That whisper... Familiar, and yet...

Whatever it was, it faded the moment he looked to the hearts. He leaned down and chose one with his tongue, and Chloe smiled when he showed it to her.

"Harder," she whispered.

Goosebumps prickled over his flesh. He held her delighted eyes, and then asked in a hoarse voice,

"Are you ready, baby?"

Taking her into the bedroom, he savored her kiss and every yearning sweep of her tongue. She held him tight, only slowing when he let her go at the edge of the bed and her feet touched the floor. Her sweater was off in a second, both of them fumbling with his pants. When they were bared, he whipped her around and held her flush, his hand breezing over her throat as he kissed her neck. Her ass pushed against his stiffening cock, causing more blood to rush there and a fire to ignite in his stomach.

"Are you mine, baby?" he whispered in her ear.

"Yes," she groaned, reaching around for his hair.

His touch skated over her stomach to between her thighs, and the wetness there made his fingers tighten on either side of her throat. "When you play with yourself tomorrow," he whispered, "or another man tries to satisfy you, whose name will you call out at your end? Tell me whose shadow you'll come for." His teeth raked over her flesh with the last of his words, and he felt goosebumps rise on her skin.

"Gavin," she moaned. "Cupid. *Eros.*"

His cock was throbbing. He groaned against her skin, trying to hold himself back from taking her too quickly. But he needed her. He needed to feel that tightening pussy. He wanted to hear that moan escaping her like she couldn't stop it.

He whirled her around again and kissed her hard, biting her lip and marking himself on her soul, and when he pulled back, he gently tugged at the roots of her hair.

"Good girl."

Chloe threw her arms around his neck, her desperate kiss landing on his lips, teeth skirting over his tongue as she consumed him. He bent them over onto the bed, and when her back hit the mattress, he finally pulled away.

"Bend over for me and grab the rails."

She placed one more kiss on his lips before doing as he said, and as she arched her ass in the air, greedily moving in front of him, he knew she knew precisely how fucking much that view would make him wild.

Gods, she was perfect.

"Spread your knees, baby—That's it—" His finger dragged up her glistening pussy. "You're so fucking beautiful," he whispered as he stroked himself and kneeled on the bed. He tapped his cock on her spread cheeks before spanking her hard.

His name escaped her lips in a moan, hips eagerly moving towards him. His finger sank slowly inside her, making him curse at the absolute drenching around his digit. He kissed her tingling red ass and bit the opposite cheek so hard that when he straightened over her, his teeth mark had indented in her flesh. A groan left her when he dragged his soaked finger over it.

"Gavin…" she begged as she shifted to look back at him.

He positioned himself steady and reached down to massage her neck, his tip tickling at her entrance. He cursed, trying to stifle how easy it would have been to come all over her beautiful ass right there.

"Do you want this?" he teased her.

"Gavin, please," she said as she pushed her hips

backwards. "Fuck me," she pleaded. "Fuck me like you'll never see me again."

The words, however simple, triggered something inside him. The knot at the pit of his stomach tightened, along with his hand in her hair.

He yanked her up the moment he slammed inside her, causing her to cry out as her head and back were bent—*craned*—and he forced her to look backwards up at him. He was buried to the hilt, and he swore she tightened even more around him when he met her upside-down gaze.

"Careful what you want," he said as she whimpered in delight at the grasp he had on her hair.

Her eyes visibly dilated, a smirk twitching on her lips. "I want you."

He groaned at the sentence and kissed her as he started moving in and out of her. His other hand dug into the bend of her hip. "Hold tight, baby," he whispered.

He released her down into the bed, his hand pushing on the small of her back and keeping her bent as he railed into her. Her slick pussy sang for him with every thrust of his cock. That beautiful fucking moan of hers muffled into the mattress, and it killed him that the fucking bed was taking that sound away from him. He pulled her up by her hair again just so he could hear her crying out.

"Fuck—*harder*—Gavin—"

Gods, she was going to send him over the edge.

He flipped her in one move, lifted her leg so that the backside of her thigh rested on his chest, and he plunged into her again. Her back arched up with every whimper and moan of his name. He slowed down, teasing her deep, watching her eyes flutter and her mouth sag.

"God, right there—*shit*—" Her fingers grabbed onto his arm, and he smiled down at her.

"Which god, baby?" he whispered as he deliberately

131

stroked that spot she liked. He held her ankle on his shoulder and reached to her clit, thumb swirling over that hardened peak, and he watched as she shook beneath him.

"Fuck—*Eros*—right there—" Her eyes met his, and he nearly lost it. "You feel so good. Don't stop. *Never* stop."

He'd never heard more beautiful words in his life.

She reached up to grab him behind the neck, her lips crashing against his as he continued moving. He could feel her reaching as he set his pace. She was a drug that he wanted to abuse and lose himself in. His forehead rested against hers, and for a moment, their shared air thickened with that need. His heart ached as she began to shake, her hands on his shoulders and gripping tightly. She was whimpering beneath him, reacting to every thrust like it was her last moment.

"Don't come yet, baby," he whispered. "I'm not done with you."

Her neck exposed with her next moan, and he knew she was straining to keep herself from spilling over.

"I'm going to—"

"Shit—"

Her walls convulsed in a manner that made all of his muscles tremble. He pulled out of her before he lost himself, and he flipped her over again and pulled her hips to him. His cock buried deep, he grabbed her around the waist and hugged her back to his chest, clutching her breast and tickling her clit. She cursed his name again as the pressure of his fingers heightened there, and he whispered against her neck,

"With me, sweet girl." He kissed her neck. "Come with me."

She bent forward again, her head lying sideways on the mattress, and he grabbed her flesh as he took them both to their ends. A high-pitched scream came from her lips, her hands holding that sheet so tight that her knuckles whitened, and when she crashed around him, he couldn't stop himself.

His release hit him like an anvil. He groaned out loudly, saying her name and slapping her ass. A cold chill washed over his entire body. Euphoria for her and the satisfied noises coming from her lips. He couldn't move for a moment, and he let himself spill completely inside her before slowly pulling himself away.

He groaned at the sight of his cum dripping out of her swollen, red pussy. He had done that. He had made her scream, made her cry, made her beg. As he dipped his fingers inside her and spread their combined juices on her ass, he heard another satisfied moan leave her throat.

"You should see our art, baby," he whispered. "I could fuck you again just to see my cum dripping out of that beautiful cunt," he said as he rubbed her thighs.

She twisted onto her back and sat her bent legs on either side of him. A vulnerability stretched over her eyes as she laid there and watched him, her breasts rising and falling with her deep breaths.

"I want to watch," she told him softly. "When I see you again, I want to see our art. I want to see your cock glistening with what you do to me."

When I see you again…

His stomach flipped that she had agreed to it. That she wanted to see him after this. That everything he was feeling was valid, and he wasn't completely losing his mind. He leaned forward, and their lips met in a needing manner as her thighs closed on either side of his hips. Her touch lingered on his stubbled cheeks, and softly, she kissed him back with a lingering promise in the way her tongue swept against his.

He crawled onto the bed atop her, making her lay back against the pillows as he hovered there, and his now unruly hair fell over his eye. She held him, her eyes searching his, as the snow continued to fall outside the window.

"What do I do to you, baby?" he asked.

The right corner of her lips quirked—so quickly that had he not been staring at her face, he would have missed it—and she pushed his hair back. "You make me want to be found."

Gavin laid awake for the remaining hours he had with her.

He remained awake and thought about tomorrow. He thought about how facing that day without her felt like the worst decision of his life.

This woman. This... this *fucking woman*...

He opened and closed his phone three times with the intention of changing his flight. He wanted to take her to breakfast, forget work and the numerous meetings he had scheduled to go over numbers the next day just to spend it with her. Even if it meant sitting on her floor and watching television while she worked.

But he respected her decision that more wasn't what she wanted. At least not now.

He would find her again.

So, he closed his phone and held her a little tighter as he formulated what he would do when it was time to leave. And when he'd finally decided, he twisted to hold her against his chest and leaned over to kiss her shoulder.

She stirred just so, her eyes fluttering open, and her lip lifted as she adjusted to tuck her hands beneath her pillow. "Hey sexy," she muttered, and he felt his own smile rise.

"Why are you still awake?" she asked in a throaty tone.

"I have to leave soon," he admitted as he ran his hand

down her hip.

"Mmm…" she shuffled closer until she was lying totally in his arms, and she laid her head on his shoulder to look up at him. "Kiss me until the last second," she whispered. "Until all I will feel at sunrise is the last of your touch on my skin."

His heart somersaulted with every word, but he held himself together. "Did you get that from a romance novel?" he teased, and that fucking smile spread wide on her lips.

"You would be surprised how beautiful minotaur erotica can be," she uttered.

His chuckle met hers, and he leaned in to kiss her. Tenderly. He wrapped her up when they parted, his lips pressing to her nose and her forehead, her cheek and her jaw, her neck and then back to her cheek, making her chuckle against him as she relaxed in his arms once again.

There was no way he was letting her go.

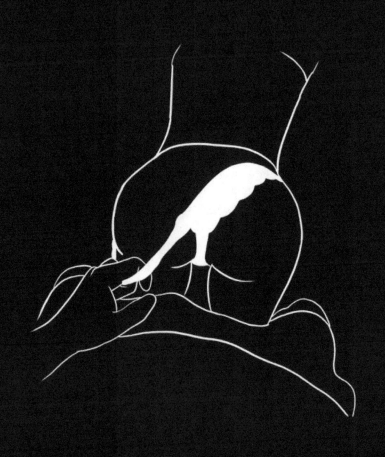

Sunlight poured through the sheer black curtains to Chloe's left.

She woke in a haze, her body aching in the best way. She stretched her arms wide, feeling her thighs twitch and a groan escape her sore throat. And as she rolled over, the remainder of Gavin's peppered scent hit her. The delicious sweet musk wafted toward her as though it had been sprayed on the fabric, causing a smile to rise on her lips.

She could still smell him on her skin... Still feel every touch burned onto her like a new tattoo. He had done as she'd asked. He had made her flesh feel as though it belonged to him with all the places he'd kissed her. Every brush of his tongue and touch of his fingers were brands of a night she wished hadn't ended, and she couldn't wait to get up and see all the marks on her from their tumble.

Her eyes fluttered open to the space he'd laid in the last few hours with her, and she almost chuckled at what she found on her pillow.

There was a note, the red handcuffs, and a candy—one that read Sweet Girl—and a warmth filled her chest at the sight of it, spreading up her neck to her ears. The paper fell open when she shifted, and the most ridiculous smile she'd ever felt spread wide on her lips at the scribble.

I'll find you.

Looking for more Gavin and Chloe?

Don't worry.
They'll be back with their own full length novel.

Coming Spring 2023

Acknowledgments

Keeping this one simple, ravens.

These two jumped into my life and now have me in a chokehold that I never want to break from. I am very excited to give them a full length novel this year and explore this Eros/Psyche retelling that I never planned for.

To Kay... bitchhhhh... I literally would not be publishing this without you! Thank you for helping me navigate this new territory with the novella format and helping me make this what it is. You the best, bestie!

To Leighann and Lex, thank you for always being there to look at a reading and helping me out when I'm stuck or need to work through something not hitting exactly right (even when I just pop it in on you at the last minute). You are both so amazing, and I cannot wait to see what this year has in store for both of you and with your books!

To Ria... You are amazing and insanely talented. This cover blows me away every time I look at it. I am so thankful I got to work with you on the cover for this book, and I can't wait to see what else you do, as well as more projects we can work together on.

To Rae, I cannot get over the NSFW line art and my new logo. You blow me away with your talent. Thank you for making this all so perfect.

To Brittany, I know you think you're not an artist, but girl!

You helped me out so much with these chapter title candy hearts! They look so good! Thank you!

To Nicole and Tiffany, thank you both so so much for jumping in and helping me out with cover and marketing directions! You both really

To Angie... thank you, thank you for being so great and helping me get this to where it needed to be! I am so appreciative of you, and I don't think I can thank you enough.

To my Nightmare of Ravens... I don't know what else to say except that you all are my favorite people, and I will never be able to repay you all for how amazing you are! This was my first jump away from Haerland, and you all have really embraced every part of this journey. Thank you for loving what I put out there and supporting me through everything!

To everyone else who has helped and supported this new endeavor for me—ARC readers, bookstagrammers, booktokers, and more... THANK YOU!

And lastly, to my amazing, amazing family that I cannot believe I am so lucky to have. Thank you for constantly supporting me and sharing and being there and just embracing this wild path and journey. Thank you for making every rare snow day into a magical time, and for every time we've made snow cream together. I know people always say 'if you like the snow, you should go find it', but it's not the same as snow at home. I love y'all.

Other Works by Jack Whitney

Now Available:

Dead Moons Rising
Book One in the Honest Scrolls Series

Flames of Promise
Book Two in the Honest Scrolls Series

The Gathering
An Honest Scrolls Novella

Sweet Girl
A Cupid Novella

Coming Soon in 2022:

Ballad (Tentative title)
A Paranormal Fantasy Romance
Book One in the Nightmares Duology
June 19th, 2022

Title T.B.D.
Book Three in the Honest Scrolls
Series Winter 2022

Jack Whitney

FALL IN LOVE WITH YOUR DARKNES
(but always take a sword)

About The Author

Jack Whitney is an adult dark fantasy and romance author out of North Carolina, US.
You can usually find her playing in dark and strange worlds. Her characters are always in charge.
She is fueled by coffee, whiskey, and shadow daydreams. If you're reading her books, they probably came with a warning label.

Welcome to the Nightmare of Ravens.

Jack also feels very weird about writing bios because she's not sure what you want to know.
She is almost always stalking social media and procrastinating, so if you would like to find her to ask more questions, please feel free.
@Jack.Whitney.Writer